THE HIGHGATE GHOST

Book 1

M.M. Gaidar

Editor – Stacey Jansen
Cover artist – FrinaArt

ISBN: 9781675277522

To my husband, Ivan
I'm not afraid of darkness when I'm with you

CONTENTS

CHAPTER 1

There's No Such Thing As Ghosts

Any more or less respected cemetery would cherish its ghost stories; however, no spirits had disturbed the life or death at London's Highgate Cemetery. No lost souls had wandered among the moss-covered gravestones, and no apparitions had spooked the visitors; that is, until recently.

Young Harmon entered the Circle of Lebanon – the heart of London's Highgate Cemetery. He pushed a wheelbarrow that jumped along the bumpy gravel road, and smiled at how joyfully the gardening tools danced on the bottom of the barrow.

Harmon liked it here at the cemetery. Usually, people were not nice to him. They called him names which he didn't understand, but they made his mother cry bitterly, so he gathered those words were bad. At the cemetery, though, all the groundsmen were nice to him. They called him Harmon-boy and made him feel like part of the family.

It was lightly drizzling. Harmon stopped and threw his head back to look up at the cedar tree sitting atop twenty chambers for the dead that formed the Lebanon Circle. That huge tree stood over the graves and crypts like an ancient god of death, watching indifferently as people came into the cemetery, but never left.

After his traditional awe-stricken tribute to the god-like tree, Harmon proceeded to trim the ferns opposite the family vault of Henry Pearse Hughs. He cut off the faded branches and put them into the wheelbarrow.

Mr Brockington's gardening shears were clipping somewhere near the Terrace Catacombs, as if measuring the time like an old and rattling grandfather clock. The clipping sound set the rhythm to Harmon's work routine. He had been dealing with the unruly vegetation until the clip-clopping of a woman's high-heeled shoes made Harmon raise his flap-eared head.

'Good evening, Miss Tesmond, Miss,' Harmon said to the young woman descending the stairs from the Terrace Catacombs.

He removed his peaked cap, as his mother had taught him to do. Miss Tesmond amiably smiled at him. She was the secretary of the cemetery's superintendent, always walking down the lanes with her sketchbook on her hours off.

'How you like the weavver today, Miss Tesmond?' Harmon asked, initiating appropriate small talk with the discussion of the elements, like any worldly and educated person would do, although he was neither this nor that.

'The rain tarnished my sketch.' The woman sighed and wrapped herself more tightly in her shawl. 'Do you want to see what I discovered today?'

Harmon put his gardening shears onto a heap of garden waste and peeked into the sketchbook Miss Tesmond opened for him. Every page was covered with drawings of the symbols and imagery from the gravestones: ivy, urn, hourglass, grapes, anchor, a chalice with a protective hand over it.

'Here is a snake biting its own tail,' she said. 'It is a symbol of eternity. And this is an inverted torch, which represents an extinguished life.'

'I like doves,' Harmon said, and with his filthy finger pointed at the sketch of one.

'Yes, doves are nice.'

Miss Tesmond squeezed his shoulder, smiling condescendingly like people always did around him.

'See you later, Harmon,' she said as she walked away.

By six o'clock, he was done with the ferns in the Circle of Lebanon. Only two more at the entrance to the Egyptian Avenue were left to do. Mr Ed Brockington came down the same stairs Miss Tesmond had ascended two hours before. He carried two squeaky buckets full of garden waste. When he came up to his younger colleague, Ed Brockington stopped and thoroughly stretched his sore back.

'It's getting dark, Harmon-boy,' the man said, taking out a tin with chewing tobacco. 'Don't want to stay here after dark.' He tucked a pinch of tobacco between his teeth and cheek. 'Not with all these stories about a ghost wandering around. Gives me the creeps.'

'I don't believe in vem ghosts.' Harmon squared his shoulders with a child-like resolution, his Cockney pronunciation, gained along with lice in the poorest neighbourhood of London, thickened, as if it was supposed to be an elixir boosting his bravery. 'Me mum says vere ain't such a fing as ghosts, and me mum is a respectable woman. We go to church every Sunday.'

The older man spat on the ground and started cleaning the caked-on dirt from his gardening tools. Harmon watched the tiny puddle of saliva, brownish from chewing tobacco, seep through the pebbles.

'Course, mate.' Ed Brockington nodded his grey head of unkempt, greasy hair, thoroughly uninterested. 'Old Tommy says he heard a woman cry near the Egyptian Avenue. But there wasn't no woman. That's how it goes. 'Course, Tommy is just an old fool and blabberer. I'd never believe it if I didn't see it with me own eyes. Just yesterday I saw the bloody thing in the Egyptian Avenue, right by the crypts.'

Harmon did not look so brave anymore. He listened, his eyes wide open, his mouth gaping. Ed Brockington threw the tools back into the bucket. 'Tommy said he was quitting his job. Can ye believe it? Good to know at least someone has their guts.' The groundsman patted his younger colleague on the shoulder. The boy's lopsided smile made him seriously question his bravery?

'So? Are ye comin'?'

'I 'ave two more bushes 'ere,' the young worker swallowed.

'Aight, then, Harmon-boy. See you tomorrow.' The groundsman pulled up his baggy pants, collected the buckets and quickly disappeared around the curve of the Lebanon Circle. The metal squeaking of the buckets that accompanied his walk died away in the distance of the lush cemetery grounds. Harmon wiped the rain droplets off his face with the back of his sleeve and proceeded to work.

Twilight descended quickly, and in the gloom of impending night, the cedar tree no longer seemed so peaceful. It towered over the cemetery, its roots clutching deep into the ground like claws. Were they penetrating the crypts? Were they troubling the dead?

Harmon hastily finished tidying the last two ferns and headed back. The Egyptian Avenue, a tunnel with rows of crypt doors on both sides, lay in his way. He stopped at the entrance, plucking up his courage to enter into the darkness. The visitors would often say fear overcame them as they found themselves between the rows of the crypts. Harmon tried to shake the superstitions out of his head and stepped into the tunnel, ready to pass through as quickly as possible, but the wheelbarrow was stubborn on the gravel. In the darkness of the tunnel, he couldn't see anything except the dull light at the end. He quickened his pace, despite the barrow wriggling in his hands like an insane cat.

A sound coming from outside the tunnel made Harmon stop dead. The sound came again. It resembled the whimpering of a child or a woman. He strained his eyes but couldn't make out anything.

'Who's vere?' he asked the pitch-black void that surrounded him.

The whimpering stopped. The gravel crunched under someone's feet. The steps were getting closer, but the boy still couldn't see anyone in the darkness. They were a couple of feet away already.

'Vere ain't such fing as ghosts!' his voice betrayed him.

He felt a raspy breath on his cheek. The hairs on the back of his head stood up. And then, out of the darkness, a ghoulish white figure advanced at him and cold fingers locked around his arm.

'No!' Harmon yelled, dropped the barrow and ran for his life.

CHAPTER 2

The Case of A Typical Gypsy

T he room was full of dreadful things. Woven dolls, bird claws, bunches of animal tails and mummified hooves. Everything Cassandra would expect to see in a gypsy's parlour. As she stood waiting for her appointment, she took in the occult atmosphere of the place with a slight smile. This trove of dreadful things did not scare her, but rather stunned her with its unscrupulous combination of some serious religious artifacts and cheap scares like bottles of fake blood or mice skeletons.

Cassandra picked up a green brass figure of Buddha from a shelf. He had such a peaceful countenance and broad smile, as though he had managed to accept the world as it is. She grinned back at him and replaced the figure on the shelf among the ones of Jesus, St Mary, Zarathustra, Santa Muerte, African tribal gods, Scandinavian gods and others who promised redemption. She was merely in her late twenties, but tempered and beaten like an old sailor who had sailed the roughest seas – she knew well enough that some things could not be redeemed, neither by people nor by gods.

Leaning on an unusually thick walking stick with a handle carved in the form of a leaping panther, Cassandra strolled around the room. The autumn weather worsened her limp.

The ventilation hole, weirdly placed in the middle of the wall and covered with a decorative screen, proved useless because it supplied not a bit of fresh air into the room. Cassandra tried to open the dirty window that was hiding behind the draping, but it was locked. Outside, London smeared the sky with the grey saliva of its factories, dragging itself into the new, twentieth century. It was October of 1900. In the article issued that day, they called Great Britain *the richest empire in the world.*

However, the other articles in the newspaper Cassandra read at breakfast revealed quite the opposite side of the empire. Thousands of paupers toiled in the workhouses; a little girl was beaten to death for stealing a rich lady's frock; women in domestic service were raped and then laughed at in the courts of justice. The upper class wrinkled their noses and turned the pages they didn't want to read, so as to not spoil their breakfasts. But who can blame them? It's not easy to see the dark when your candles and diamonds are shining so brightly. Neither can you hear the lament through the jolly tunes of the concert halls.

As Cassandra decided to make herself comfortable to massage her leg in the only armchair amidst the occult junk, the mistress of the house came in. She appeared dramatically from a waterfall of beads that covered the doorway between two rooms. The mistress was a short gypsy, around fifty, whose every move was accompanied by the chiming of her bracelets and earrings. It was impossible to imagine a more gypsy-looking gypsy.

'My apologies that I've kept you waiting Miss –' she said with an accent whose origin was hard to identify.

'It's Miss Clarke.' Cassandra used a false name as she always did when she went undercover. The gypsy invited her into the adjacent room with a gesture of her hand, and the guest entered.

'I think you know my name.'

Cassandra nodded. Gypsy Hester was a rather well-known persona in London, with certain circles of people.

Here, it was even stuffier and harder to breathe. The light struggled through half-closed shutters and fell to the floor, exhausted, forming a very thin line of illumination. Candles occupied every vacant spot. They melted on the mantelpiece and formed long white beards of hardened wax that almost reached the floor.

With another florid gesture, the gypsy invited Cassandra to sit at the table covered with a velvet tablecloth. The woman sat across from her client, and put her hands, fingers adorned with rings, on the table. Her sharp, pitch-black eyes studied the client.

'So why are you here, dear?' the gypsy asked.

Cassandra took off her sunglasses with the round green lenses and put them aside. She peeled the gloves off her hands and asked, 'Do you mind if I smoke?'

The mistress of the house allowed her with a blink of her eyes. The client took out a cigarette box and lit a cigarette from a ritual candle.

'A friend of mine, Mrs Roberts, has assured me that you can answer the question that haunts me,' Cassandra said.

'Ah, Mrs Roberts! Such a lovely woman,' the gypsy grinned, revealing brown and broken teeth. 'What is your question, dear?'

'When I was a little girl, I had an accident.' She pulled at the cigarette, a veil of smoke hanging between them. 'The doctors say my child's brain was trying to cope with the trauma; that's why it blocked the memories. But now I want to remember that day.'

The gypsy nodded to every word.

'And you want old Gypsy Hester to help you recover your memory? Give me your hand.'

The gypsy placed Cassandra's hand on her wrinkled forehead. She closed her eyes and started whispering incantations.

'I see darkness and suffering. You were an unhappy child. Many appalling things happened to you. Every day spent in your family home was bleak. And then... I see an injury. You fell.'

'This is exactly what I want to know about. How did it happen?' Cassandra asked.

The gypsy winced as though trying hard to see the answer.

'I can't see. Dark energy obscures that day.'

'What does this mean?'

She opened her eyes and patted her client's hand with sympathy.

'It seems, dear, you need to order a cleansing ritual. It will enable me to see into your past. And, since you are Mrs Roberts's friend, it will be just ten shillings for you.'

Cassandra produced the required sum from her purse. The coins appeared on the velvet tablecloth.

'No, no, no, no, my dear,' the gypsy said. 'These things need preparation. Come in a week.'

'Oh, it's very convenient, of course,' the client chuckled. 'But unimpressive.'

'What is that?'

Cassandra sat back in her armchair. The false identity of a damsel in distress vanished, together with the cigarette smoke she puffed in the gypsy's face.

'Unhappy child, problems in the family. This could be applied to any troubled soul who comes to you. Happy people don't seek your help, do they? As for the injury and my fall, it doesn't take a genius to come to this conclusion,' she nodded at her walking stick.

'I don't understand. Who are you?' Hester demanded.

'You watch your clients through that ventilation hole.' Cassandra pointed with her walking stick at the decorative screen that was covering the misplaced ventilation. 'You observe how they behave. You study them before inviting them in. Then you load their minds with some easily predictable nonsense and offer them a cleansing ritual. Before their next visit, you do a little research about who they are. The next time they come, you are ready to manipulate them, drawing out of them new, unsolved problems, traumas and money, over and over again, until they can't take a step without consulting with you.'

The gypsy crossed her hands.

'What is it you want?' she asked, her voice suddenly Irish.

'I want you, you old manipulative witch, to leave Mrs Roberts alone,' she said calmly, removing a tobacco bit from the tip of her tongue.

'Or what?'

'Or I'll expose you. I'm sure the newspapers will find your story ravishing.'

'Pfft. You don't have anything on me.'

'Come on, Hester. I've also done some research. Or maybe you prefer me to call you Mrs Kyra O'Brien?'

The woman's face melted.

'If you don't want to learn firsthand about my method, you'll leave Mrs Roberts alone and return all the money you've ever tricked out of her.' Cassandra stood up and put her cigarette out in Hester's tray full of ritual coins. She turned over the top card in the Tarot deck – it was bearing the image of The Hanged Man.

'If I'm not mistaken, if upright, this card means a dead-end situation, an impasse,' she commented. 'Cards never lie, do they?'

'Who the hell are you?'

'Cassandra Ayers. A private detective at your service.' She tossed her business card on the table. 'I investigate the so-called supernatural cases.'

* * *

Mrs Roberts, the mistress of the house, was a compassionate woman; one could guess it by her eyes – they teared up easily. A sad smile was always pinned to this woman's lips, as if not to let her face crumble. She poured a cup of tea for Cassandra in her usual melancholic manner.

'Help yourself to some biscuits,' said Mrs Roberts, putting the cake stand closer to her guest.

Cassandra took a sip of tea. Pecking at a biscuit, she looked around the green drawing room in Mrs Roberts's townhouse – elegantly furnished, with the mahogany furniture polished to a gleam. A bay window overlooked a picturesque, lush English garden so beautiful it overshadowed the refined paintings on the walls. A pair of sand-coloured Corgis were frolicking in the sun. An idyllic picture. Yet, nothing was idyllic in this grief-ridden house.

Everything here made an impression of frailty: lukewarm

tea, sugarless biscuits, dim light. Mrs Roberts herself held a cup of tea on a saucer but seemed to have no intention of drinking it, her unfocused gaze wandering somewhere in the shadows of the garden outside. Her son, Charles, was the only source of energy; waiting for the formalities to be over, he drummed his fingers on the armrest of the chair. He was dying to move on to the question that actually brought Cassandra here.

'So, Miss Ayers, do you have any news for us?' he asked.

His mother only now realised why she was here and what was happening. Her gaze slowly, like an emaciated salt-mine labourer, travelled from the window to their visitor.

'I do. I have been to Gypsy Hester's place,' Cassandra said, replacing her cup in the saucer and picking up her satchel from the floor.

'And?' Charles leaned forward.

Feeling acutely that the mother and son were expecting to hear the opposite of what she was about to say, Cassandra minced her words.

'I doubt the woman has the talent she claims she has.'

Charles sat back and sighed with relief.

'As I've suspected all along.'

'Oh, no! That can't be, my dear,' Mrs Roberts said with a sad smile and teary eyes. 'Hester knows things. Believe me, she does.'

Her son bulged his eyes at her in disbelief.

'Mother, she has been fooling you all this time.'

'But how did she know all those facts about my poor late husband? That he was a military man? That he got injured in the Crimean War?'

Cassandra pulled a folder out of her bag and removed some newspaper clippings.

'I'm sorry, Mrs Roberts, but this woman is not even a gypsy. She's Irish. Her name is Kyra O'Brien. She served in several houses as a governess,' she said, extending the folder to Mrs Roberts. 'She is a highly manipulative character. In each of the households in which she was employed, she managed to talk other servants into her schemes, stealing jewellery with the hands of others. She was caught only because one of them turned her in to avoid imprisonment. Kyra O'Brien spent five years in gaol in Dublin. It seems she's reinvented herself here in London as Gypsy Hester. A real prodigy she is. To persuade the client she is gifted with clairvoyance, she puts together a dossier about them that includes everything she can learn about their past. When you've made someone believe you can see into their past, it's not hard to make them believe you can actually read their future, as well. We have to give her credit. Even though she is not a real clairvoyant, O'Brien can read people – a gift as rare as palm reading.'

Mrs Roberts took up a clipping with a photo of Kyra O'Brien, so astonished, she couldn't speak. Her son gave Cassandra a thankful nod.

There was always a painful end to any investigation. Clients hire a private detective and pay them money just to be hurt by the truth. The pain was inevitable but still unexpected, as if they were going to cut off their own finger with the hope it would not cripple them.

'There's one more thing,' Cassandra added, retrieving a purse full of money from her bag and putting it on the table next to the porcelain service and biscuits.

'Here's every penny you paid to Hester. She won't bother you again.'

'My word, you are a magician, Miss Ayers, you truly are!' Charles said, slapping his knee in delight. 'Just look what you've pulled out of the hat!'

His mother didn't utter a word, still holding the newspaper clippings in her hands. Cassandra favoured Charles with a reserved smile and rose to her feet. Charles sprang up, too. Mrs Roberts raised her puffy eyes to the messenger who had just crushed her little world of hope.

'You are leaving already? But you haven't finished your tea.'

'I have another call to make,' the detective lied. She simply wanted to get away from this place soaked with grief. The all consuming unhappiness was like a narcotic she used to abuse, but was now afraid to be intoxicated by it again. In this drawing room, she felt like she was back at home, at that bleak place, a little girl again, scared and miserable, and it made her sick. 'Good day!'

Charles opened the door for her.

'Miss Ayers!' Mrs Roberts called out. 'Wait, please.'

Her gait was soft and quiet as she approached, her fists clenched, lips pursed, as if she was putting a tremendous amount of effort into keeping inside all that could escape. This petite woman, tiny like a sparrow, came up to Cassandra and looked her in the eye.

'I've heard you investigate such cases, the supernatural ones, so I was wondering, maybe you know.' She was ashamed to talk. 'Do you think they know how sorry we are? I mean, those who are not with us anymore.'

Compassion for this sorrowful woman choked the detective. People often deceive themselves, thinking that someone like Cassandra knew something that was beyond their understanding. More than anything in the world, Cassandra wanted to know, wanted to tame Mrs Roberts's pain, and her own pain, as well. What would be the harm if she told a small lie to comfort the woman? She wanted to, but the words stuck in her throat.

'No. I don't think they do,' Cassandra replied. 'I'm sorry.'

* * *

On the way to her rented room in Soho, Cassandra came across a dead dog lying in the gutter. Drawn by the sight, she moved closer. Strange anxiety always overwhelmed her when she saw dead things. This small, lifeless creature was a whole cosmos of non-existence that absorbed her. The absence of life right in the middle of a bustling street. What could be more grotesque? How could death be so omnipresent amidst the surrounding rave of life?

But the truth is, death was always there, everywhere, casting shadows on unsuspecting living beings. Sometimes it seemed to Cassandra that death was even trying to communicate with her, sending her veiled signs of his presence, never leaving her alone, like a lover consumed with a desire that can never be quenched. Neither the walls of her home nor the locks on the doors stopped him from visiting whenever it pleased him and holding Cassandra in his icy embrace.

The house where the detective lodged was not much of a protection from anything, though. It looked like a rotten tooth – blackened and decaying. The landlord, a philanthropist who read Tolstoy and considered him his god, allowed many poor souls into his house, every free spot given to a dweller in need, and to beggars, squanderers and idlers. They all hated London, this big whore, with a prim facade but indecent interiors. And London sincerely hated them back.

Even under the stairs in this charitable Babylon there lived a family: Mrs Cox and her brood of noisy children. When Cassandra entered the vestibule, Mrs Cox, red-faced and sweaty, was washing the old yellow linen in the filthy water that would not clean the dirt even off the road, let alone clothes. The water looked like the entire house had already bathed in it. The sour reek of the soaking underwear was overpowering.

'Hi, love.' Mrs Cox blew away a mousy strand of hair obscuring her view. 'Give me your stuff. I'll wash it for you.'

'Oh, no, thank you. I took mine to the Chinese washhouse,' Cassandra lied. In fact, a week ago, Uncle Zhang Yong's washhouse was burnt to the ground and they had hired her to investigate. It turned out not easy to prove that the fire was started by the competitors and had nothing to do with the curse the Yongs believed in, because their washhouse had burnt four times over the last year.

Cassandra quickened her pace – the smell of the soaking underwear was terrible and she wanted to escape, but the children from under the stairs had already spotted her and dashed after her like a pack of retrievers after a fox.

'Miss Ayers! Miss Ayers! Look!' they all shouted and started making faces, each trying to outdo the other. Their grimy faces contorted into hideous expressions that could make the gargoyles from Notre-Dame de Paris envious.

'Who is the scariest of all?' they asked.

'Don't mind them, love,' their mother said. 'Let her be, you little rascals.' She swatted the air around them with a wet nightgown, but she wasn't angry with them. Not really. She stuck the nightgown into the mangle and shooed away the youngest girl who was poking her little fingers between the two rollers of the machine.

'Look, Miss Ayers! Look!' the children didn't give up, showing faces at her.

Cassandra stopped at the bottom of the stairs to give the children's artistic attempts a professional look. Harry, the eldest, had succeeded in stretching his ears and popping his eyes out so much that he deserved a reward. The detective produced a coin from her purse and gave it to Harry. The boy raised his arms in a victorious gesture.

'Not fair!' the other children moaned.

'Monkeyface is not even scary!' was someone's opinion.

'Ya spoiling them little beasts, Miss Ayers,' their mother said with a smile, but didn't protest the money donation.

With a smirk nudged into the corner of her mouth, Cassandra made her way upstairs. The steps were creaking like an old man's joints. Even though she could afford to rent rooms in a place much more decent than this one, where no one slept under the stairs, where there were no foul smells from unwashed bodies, and smiles were not all rotten, she chose to be here, in a place such as this, as if winning the affections of these sorts of people was a personal crusade for her, an aristocrat by birth. Some years ago, she ran away from her family mansion with no money under her belt, and she now lived off what she earned from investigating these petty cases.

The dwelling no longer struck her as miserable or ugly. She knew firsthand there was nothing sincere in the splendour of the best London drawing rooms: beneath the gilt, it was all putridity. Here it was at least truthfully wretched.

At the door to her room, Cassandra stepped on the envelope that someone had left there. She bent and picked it up. The familiar handwriting made her eyes roll – it was signed by Lydia Ayers, Cassandra's stepmother, and sent from Caxton Hall, the family mansion. The detective unlocked the door and entered, anticipating the upsetting read.

Within the four walls of her room, whose colour was hard to determine under the soot from the gas lamps, there was scant furnishing: a bed, desk, chair, chest of drawers and a tiny vanity. Books and Cassandra's scribbling on pieces of paper piled up on every vacant spot.

As soon as she kicked off her shoes and took off the little hat attached to her hair with a huge pin, the detective opened the envelope from Caxton Hall. These letters she preferred to read while standing so that she could quickly toss them in the fireplace.

Lydia's handwriting was impeccable, but something was annoying about how diligently and deliberately that woman wrote the words that always cut deeper than any blade.

My dearest Cassandra,

It is hard for me to fathom the degree of your spite towards your own family that has not wronged you in any way.

Cassandra scoffed in disbelief.

Whatever you contrived in your head against your father, you could pay him a visit now, when he is gravely ill. Or at the very least send him a photograph of yourself to please his wearied heart.

'The man doesn't have a heart,' Cassandra mumbled.

She crumpled up the letter and tossed it into the fireplace. On the mantle there sat a photograph of her mother, Evelyn Ayers, who died many years ago, leaving her daughter, only six back then, with little to remember. The photograph showed the woman in her prime, just married, her beauty not yet clouded by the imminent tragedy. She was dressed in flowing silk and, with the airs of a theatre actress, leaned graciously on a carved chair. Her hands rested on the back of the chair, making prominent the only piece of jewellery that adorned her fingers: a band of gold with three rubies set amidst a sprinkle of diamonds. She looked so full of life in that picture. What could have happened to her? What could have gone wrong? These were the questions that had been haunting Cassandra all her life.

Soon, the night drew its black curtains over London. In the ghostly light of a single gas lamp, she felt vulnerable. Damaged shadows lurked around the corners and sneaked up on her, bringing back unwanted memories. The house moaned as it struggled against the wind, or maybe it gasped from fear of something that hid in the dark.

Cassandra put on her dressing robe. Unable to concentrate, she set aside the research she had been carrying for some years now. The books lay deserted: *Interpretation of Dreams, A Manual of Diseases of the Nervous System, The Causes of Hallucinations, Lethargy, Stupor or Coma.*

Gypsy Hester was right about one thing: Cassandra did fall – from the second storey of her family mansion. So traumatic was the incident, her memories of it have been lost almost completely since that day. After all these years, she hadn't approached the answer to what had happened to her, not by even an inch. Her memories, whatever was left of them, were punctuated by images and sensations from the past that did not make any sense.

She massaged her leg, stiff after a whole day of walking. The only thing that helped her lull the searing pain was opium. A pleasant rush of excitement engulfed her as she commenced her ritual. She took out the tray outfitted with paraphernalia for smoking opium and placed it on the bedside table. Her hands trembled as she lit *yen dong*, the opium lamp. The substance was good for taming her inner demons, as well.

After she'd smoked her pipe, she lay in bed, enveloped in the clouds of intoxicating smoke. Cassandra gave in and drifted away – into the world of her shattered memories.

She was thirteen again, asleep in her bed, when suddenly she awoke with the feeling something else was present in the room.

Cassie sat up, fuzzy with sleep, uncertain if she was still sleeping or awake. She could hear indistinct voices and muffled screams but could not place where they were coming from. It seemed the walls themselves were screaming. She scrambled out of her bed and peeked out of her room.

The corridor at night always scared her. It was long, with no windows, and lit only by a couple of dim gas lamps. It seemed endless, like a tunnel leading to hell. Cassie walked barefoot on the cold wooden floor, her ears sharper than ever, picking up every sound.

Oddly, all the doors gaped open, as if inviting Cassie into the guest rooms that were normally shut tight, not having seen guests in many years.

As she crept by the first room, Cassie turned slowly to look inside. Her heart thudded leadenly as she beheld a woman in a black gown standing in the middle of the room, staring into dark nothingness before her. Cassie turned away, petrified, and edged farther down the corridor. The same woman appeared in the next room. Cassie's eyes only touched on the dark silhouette before hurrying away. The woman insistently reappeared in each room as Cassie scurried past. Repeatedly, the grim figure took up a stool and placed it in front of herself.

Unable to breathe for fear, Cassie neared the last guest room just in time to witness what she had already witnessed once before: the woman climbed up on the stool, put a noose around her neck, and took a step into oblivion. Cassie watched her dangling by the rope, her feet twitching. It was her mother.

Weeping, little Cassie fled, the whispers and screams following her from behind the walls. When she reached the Family Gallery, she stopped and tried to recover her breath under the grand chandelier the size of a Christmas tree glimmering in the dark.

Hideous, disfigured faces stared down at her from an old tapestry. A figure entered her peripheral sight. Cassie wheeled to see who it was, only to be pushed by someone strong and violent. She flew through the air over the banister and fell onto the marble floor of the hall below.

That night turned Cassandra into a cripple for life, but she still couldn't find an explanation for what had really happened to her. Was it a dream or reality? Was it something she saw or something her imagination conjured to fill in the blank spaces? The only thing she knew for sure – her mother had taken her own life more than twenty years ago, and six years after this, Cassandra fell off the gallery, surviving by sheer chance. Something vile wandered within the walls of the bleak Ayers mansion, Caxton Hall.

CHAPTER 3

Blonde Curls, Ruffs and Flowers,
but No Chichen Itza

One bright autumn morning, shortly after Gypsy Hester's case, Cassandra sauntered down bustling Fleet Street. She was hiding her thoughtful gaze behind the green lenses of her sunglasses, trying to seem as "normal" as all the people around her. Normality provided her with a retreat from the gruelling everyday struggle of being herself.

Yet, she was not normal by any stretch of even a mediocre imagination. Her choice of "inappropriate" relations, love of weird things, smoking, aggressive perfume, dark robes and grim poetry, sketches of dead creatures and the filth of the world marked her as "peculiar" – that was the word her stepmother, Lydia, used to describe her. The combination of all that, topped with her mysterious magnetism, made some in the idle crowd of passers-by turn their heads.

Cassandra stopped in front of the four-storey building whose elegant plaque declared The London. Not the type of place she could usually afford; the ones she frequented looked like a cheap tart aspiring to be a lady. The London, on the contrary, was an establishment where all the waiters, crisply uniformed, with a healthy dollop of pomade, served excellent food with just the right level of service. Exactly the kind of place her school friend Lavinia would pick for their first get-together after her return from a long honeymoon on the Continent.

No matter how much Cassandra tried not to care, she felt a pang at recollecting how she had not been invited to Lavinia's wedding. She reminded herself that it was not Lavinia's fault, after all. The reason why Cassandra had become an unwelcome guest was her friend's fiancé, now husband, Captain William Drummond. The man loathed Cassandra and everything she stood for. A social climber, Captain Drummond took pains to ensure he and his new wife travelled in the right circles. Drummond found it particularly galling that Cassandra, coming as she did from aristocratic stock, should deliberately turn her back on the very things he craved with every fibre of his being: status, money, power.

With a slight and socially appropriate smile pinned to her lips, that was neither approving nor the opposite of that, Cassandra entered. The hall of the restaurant, spacious and full of light, was filled with a murmurous drone of the people talking at their tables. The gentlemen and ladies dined in style and enjoyed lively conversations. It was a realm prim and proper to the most minuscule rosebud painted on the platter, a realm where no one said what they truly thought because the truth was considered vulgar.

The sight of the great hall brought back sentiments that still made Cassandra wonder if it was because of her intemperate youth she ran away from home, and the privileged society into which she was born; after all, she had everything for an affluent life. But the sentiment did not last long. She remembered quite well, those were not shallow conversations or unfriendly stares that drove her away. The reason was much darker. So dark in fact, she did not dare think of it. All explanations had been replaced by one scary word – *father*.

A moment later, after a deep breath and a reinforced smile, Cassandra looked around. The vestibule was decorated with Empire-style furniture and vases full of late peonies, the last of the season. The ceiling was so high that Cassandra felt a little taller herself, as though a lot of spare room above her head let her uncurl to her utmost height.

'Welcome to The London, madam. Do you have a table reserved?' the Maitre d' asked with a court drawl.

'My friend Mrs Drummond is waiting for me.'

Her eyes travelled around the hall until she spied an elegantly dressed young lady waving her hand at Cassandra.

'I can see her.'

Swerving between the small round tables scattered around the dining hall, Cassandra limped towards her old school friend – a beauty with blonde curls. Her dress was a mass of ruffs and flowers which enhanced her figure and made her resemble a woman from a Renoir painting. The two friends embraced for a polite amount of time between old friends, before releasing each other just long enough to examine the other's deportment, and then hugging again.

'My dearest, dearest friend!' Lavinia cried.

'Why, you look like a proper high society lady now, Lavinia! Or should I say Mrs Drummond?'

Lavinia chuckled. They sat at the table, holding hands and paying no attention to the waiter who had brought them menus. The young man promised to return soon.

Cassandra took a deep breath before asking: 'So..?'

'So...' Lavinia dwelt on the word, coquettishly holding her friend in suspense. 'William and I – uh, we are doing just fine. He is a good husband. Very gentle and thoughtful. And generous, too. He is a real gentleman.'

'My! That's a lot of compliments. Well, if he makes you happy...'

Lavinia's smile turned just a fraction more bitter.

'Come on, Cassie. You know I'm not like you. I can take pleasure in simple family life.'

Cassandra knew the others called her *frigid* behind her back. Everyone believed she, this weird woman, chose to not need a family, while, in fact, she was never given the privilege of a choice. She just accepted from life what she was given – a family she best stay away from. No one needed her, and she was forced to substitute the word *freedom* in place of the word *loneliness*; at least being free was not so pathetic as being lonely. Yet, a woman's freedom in a world owned by men differed very subtly from isolation. Unmarried and making her own living, she wasn't welcome in many proper houses.

Whatever truth was in her head and on her tongue was quickly dismissed as improper before Cassandra playfully winked and said, 'Well, tell me all about the delights of the family life you've discovered.'

Lavinia nearly burst at the seams and slightly slapped Cassandra on her wrist for being naughty. And of course, there was a lot to say. About their trip to Italy, about romance, breakfasts in Venice, holding hands, dancing, paying visits to the finest families. The insufferably detailed account of a person in love. Cassandra allowed Lavinia's talk to flow freely, while memories of the past inundated her even more intensely.

In the years they spent together as children at the girls' boarding school, Cassandra and Lavinia dreamt of freedom and adventure; however, their dreams of going to Chichen Itza, receiving an education at Oxford, or taking up the profession of journalism were fine for adolescent girls giggling together under the covers long after midnight, but as the girls grew up, their society had other, very different ideas in store for them.

Lavinia's rebellion against the constraints of society did not last long after she reached adolescence. Shortly after her debut into society and a couple of cotillions, she fell for William Drummond, a captain in the British Army. He was stiff like a mop, with a silly handlebar moustache that he pinched all the time with a look of importance. Such a self-loving prig. But only in Cassandra's eyes. She did not say a word, afraid of losing her friend, but the silence she kept said enough.

Now Lavinia, sitting across from her, cackled about her honeymoon and the "funny" things William said. Chichen Itza had been forgotten and discarded as waste; the friendship was discarded as an uncomfortable chair. Lavinia did not belong with her friend anymore.

The waiter returned ready to take their orders.

'A breaded veal cutlet with peas and potato, French cream pie, and a glass of claret,' Lavinia ordered.

The waiter shifted his look to Cassandra.

'I'll have the same.'

'Two plates of breaded veal cutlet with peas and potato, French cream pie, and two glasses of claret. Will that be all?'

'Make it two for me,' said Cassandra. 'The wine.'

The waiter nodded his approval and left.

'I hear you are a real detective now,' Lavinia said, her eyes wide open with fascination.

'I'm nothing of the kind. People ask me to investigate some simple things for them and I do so.'

'No need to be modest. You are a modern woman earning her own living. Isn't it what you've always wanted?' Was there a pinch of irony in Lavinia's words?

'That's something I really care about. If that's what you mean.'

'I'm glad. If it makes you happy,' Lavinia copied Cassandra's words from before and smiled cheekily.

'It does,' the detective admitted, suddenly relieved to learn that amidst all the misery there was something to cling to.

The wine arrived.

'To the old days,' Lavinia said, holding her glass up for a toast.

A little taken by surprise with this sentimentality, Cassandra raised her glass, too.

'And to the old dreams,' she chimed in.

The two friends took a sip. Lavinia licked the wine from her lips and asked, 'By the way, do you remember my uncle, the superintendent of Highgate Cemetery?'

'The one who always invited you for Christmas?'

'Yes, Uncle Redlaw, my mother's brother.'

'Of course, I remember him. He sent us the most delicious fudge. How is he?'

'In good health. Thank you. I saw him a couple of days ago and mentioned that you'd become a private investigator. He said he would have the use of your services.'

'Oh?'

The waiter returned with their order, and they were forced to hold back their conversation. While the cutlets on the fine plates made their way onto the table, Cassandra was dying to know what her friend meant by her uncle needing her as a detective.

Finally, when the waiter was gone and Lavinia armed herself with a fork and knife, the talk resumed. 'You see, Uncle Redlaw says it has been hard for him to retain gardeners and groundsmen lately. It seems they all have handed in their notices.'

'And he wants me to find out why?' Cassandra took a guess.

'Oh, he knows why. They're saying there is a ghost haunting Highgate. Complete hogwash if you ask me. But that's your domain, right?'

CHAPTER 4

Highgate Cemetery

Cassandra threw her head back to fully take in the imposing chapels flanking the entrance to Highgate Cemetery. The sombre sight gave her an unpleasant feeling, a stirring of her innermost monsters. Was there really a ghost roaming the grounds? Was it truly a manifestation of the afterlife? Many people had claimed to have witnessed supernatural occurrences, but never had those claims proven to be true. While the idea seemed incredible that this time the ghost was not some trickster in a white bed sheet, the hardened detective secretly hoped for it to be true. Even though she didn't believe in ghosts, she truly wanted to believe – at least in something.

A well-dressed man walked towards her through an archway between the two chapels. He was a tall man of around fifty, wearing all black but smiling broadly despite his dark clothes, a smile big enough to seem inappropriate given the surroundings and an attire normally reserved for death and mourning.

'Ah! Miss Ayers. Welcome to Highgate Cemetery. It is a rare occasion I can welcome somebody as a guest in this realm of decay and grief,' he said, doffing his top hat. 'John Redlaw, superintendent.'

Cassandra shook hands with him and said, 'I hear you've got some unwelcome visitors here.'

'Yes. Believe it or not, all my workers are terrified to set foot on the cemetery grounds. They have either seen or heard something. And last night another terrible thing happened! Let me show you.'

They entered the archway together. A priest stepped out from one of the doors leading to the Anglican chapel. He was a stout and flabby man in his mid-sixties, with a glistening bald patch and mottled skin on the top of his head.

'This is Reverend Gummidge,' Mr Redlaw said. The reverend stopped. 'May I introduce Miss Ayers.'

'Ah, the ghost huntress!' Reverend Gummidge said, holding fast to his Bible with both hands as if afraid to lose them to this woman he obviously thought was not to be trusted. He said nothing more before making himself scarce.

Mr Redlaw gave Cassandra an apologetic look. 'Not everyone approves of my decision to bring you here.'

'Don't worry, Mr Redlaw. I'm used to this attitude.'

'I'm sorry you have to say that. I think what you're doing is absolutely fascinating.'

'Working the supernatural cases?'

'Well, that too. But mostly your unyielding will to live the life you chose for yourself. It must be tough.'

Cassandra stopped and gave Mr Redlaw a long and intent gaze as if she was trying to understand if he was not making fun of her. His features softened with a fatherly smile.

'Thank you for saying that,' she finally answered. 'It means a lot to me.'

'Of course.' He offered to proceed with a gesture of his hand and continued. 'Lavinia wouldn't stop talking about you when you both were little girls. Unfortunately, the poor thing didn't have a father, as you must know.'

'Yes. A tragic story. It's so sad he died just before his child was born and was never able to meet her.'

'Quite so. Well, I always considered myself obliged to give her my attention and advice whenever I felt it was needed. I supported her wish to enter the university, which was inspired by you I suppose. But it was not meant to happen.'

Cassandra couldn't find any comforting words that wouldn't come across as a banality she actually didn't believe in, so she said, 'On the other hand, her life will be settled and calm.'

'That's right. However, settled and calm are not synonymous with happy. No. People don't choose settled and calm because they believe it is good for them. They choose it because it is easy.'

'Are you sure, though, that people really choose what their lives will be?' she asked. 'Choices are difficult.'

'But what does a life without choice make us if not slaves?'

'Do you always offer your guests a philosophical discussion?' Cassandra smiled.

'Heavens, no. I'd then have no guests, at all.' Mr Redlaw's hearty laughter bounced off the cobbled courtyard and echoed in the Colonnade with the fifteen arches.

The route to the higher cemetery grounds ran through the Colonnade and up a flight of stairs. As they climbed the steps, the tombs and gravestones emerged before them. Cassandra deeply inhaled the tart tang of autumnal decay and wet ground – the smell of nostalgia and anxiety.

The lanes of the cemetery, cocooned within the canopy of trees entwined together, were covered with a slippery carpet of foliage and mud. The rows of tombs, silent monuments of perished lives, rose on both sides of the lanes. Everything was dead here, but Cassandra had a feeling this wasn't an absolute void. For her, there was something elusively present in the sepulchral void of non-existence. Something she couldn't grasp or explain. A cold shiver slithered up the back of her head and into her hair.

'We found it this morning,' Mr Redlaw said when they arrived at a grave that had been dug up. It resembled a black mouth open in a silent scream of terror. The detective stared at it, examining it, unable to take her eyes away from its ungodly nakedness.

'People are saying it is the ghost's doing,' Mr Redlaw added, and chuckled at this outlandish proposal.

The coffin had been opened, too, exposing the skeleton

within to the cold drizzle that seeped through the leaves of the canopy. Cassandra crouched and inspected the edges of the hole in the ground. The mud bore the marks of a shovel. She let out a sigh of slight disappointment.

'So what do you say?' Mr Redlaw asked.

'That your ghost has a taste for vandalism.' She rose to her feet. 'And is quite capable of using the gardening tools.'

She took out a pocketbook and a slate pencil and wrote down the particulars from the headstone: *Nathan Ricket. Born 3 May 1820. Died 15 October 1891.* The grave was rather plain: a symbol of a chalice with a protective hand covering it served as its only decoration.

'What are you going to do with this?' the superintendent asked.

'Find out who this man was and try to understand why the ghost decided to go poking into this poor chap's grave.'

'It means you are taking this case?'

Cassandra gave him a reassuring nod.

'Then you must see the other grave.'

'The other grave?'

'Yes. Two graves were dug up overnight. Can't even think how they managed to pull this off. Of course, if the guard hadn't quit… The other one is farther down the lane. Come on. I'll take you there.'

They walked deeper into the cemetery, until a flash of a photo camera and a loud explosion of flash powder stole their attention. Off the main lane, a young man stood behind a camera mounted on a tripod. He was taking pictures of the other defiled grave.

'Oh, he's still here.' Mr Redlaw did not sound pleased.

Cassandra and Mr Redlaw swerved from the lane and proceeded deeper into the thickets of the park where the looted grave sat like a nude model for the photographer.

'Who is he?' Cassandra asked.

'The son of Lord Salisbury. I couldn't refuse him a visit.'

'May I ask what you're doing, sir?' The detective's voice

spooked the photographer and he turned to face them.

He regained his composure instantaneously and smiled, proudly patting his three-legged tool of the trade as though it were his horse.

'I'm catching the ghost on camera,' he said in a surprised tone as if it was obvious.

Cassandra scoffed. She looked at the numerous footprints in the soil around the grave, then at the man's shoes covered in dirt. The photographer followed her stare.

'Do you realise that you've ruined the crime scene?' The detective's voice was stern.

The stranger flashed an even broader smile at her.

'Wait a minute. You are Cassandra Ayers, am I right? The Great Debunker? Valentine Duvar.' He readily extended his hand for a handshake, but the woman brushed past him. She approached the grave that was in the same dire state as the first one she inspected. 'Are you here to investigate?'

'Listen, Mr Duvar. I have little patience for cranks who sniff around and chase apparitions while I'm doing my job, even if they are sons of somebody.' Cassandra examined the edges of the hole.

'Ah. I see. You don't care for a bit of healthy nepotism?' Valentine chortled.

'I don't, no.'

She took out her pocketbook and slate pencil and wrote down the particulars from the headstone: *Omer Ingleton. Born 16 November 1813. Died 23 February 1889.*

'They were peers. Perhaps they knew each other?' Cassandra mumbled under her breath.

'Come again,' Mr Redlaw said, coming closer.

'Do you know if these men knew each other?'

'I only took over the position of superintendent two years ago. I'm afraid I have no knowledge of the people buried before that.'

'Do you preserve any records of their immediate family?' Cassandra asked. She moved the foliage aside with her cane to see if there were any footprints, but, as she expected, the morning rain had washed them away.

'My secretary, Miss Tesmond, may be able to help with that.'

'Good.'

'We are not that different, you know,' Valentine edged in, watching with curiosity what the detective was doing. 'I'm also looking for the truth.'

'For the truth?' she asked incredulously. 'Where? Behind smoke and mirrors?'

After a closer look at the headstone, Cassandra noticed it was engraved with the same symbol as that on Nathan Ricket's headstone. She made a rough sketch of it.

'Is this a common image to be engraved on headstones?'

Mr Redlaw strained his eyes to see it better.

'No. Haven't seen anything of this kind before. I'm not too attentive, though. You shouldn't rely on me.'

Cassandra added the last touches to her sketch while Valentine was watching over her shoulder.

'This symbol...' he said. 'Looks familiar.'

The detective favoured him with a get-lost look and shut her pocketbook with a loud clap. Her antagonism did not discourage Mr Duvar.

'I've heard you specialize in mysterious cases, Miss Ayers. But you still do not believe in ghosts?' he asked.

'Not in those that can handle a spade.'

She pointed at the edges of the defiled grave.

'You see these marks? They are clearly left by a spade.'

Mr Redlaw's top hat moved up as his eyebrows arched. Duvar wasn't persuaded by this.

'I say!' the superintendent said.

Cassandra shoved her pocketbook and pencil back into her satchel.

'Believe me, Mr Redlaw. There's nothing more mysterious than human nature. There's no explanation as to why they pursue the most nonsensical theories.'

Valentine, who was preparing his camera for another shot,

chuckled at the sarcasm in her words.

Mr Redlaw offered Cassandra his hand as they clambered up a wet slope. The mud smacked like the toothless mouth of a cadaver every time she extracted her walking stick from its suctioning thickness.

'Let me show you the other corners of the cemetery, so you feel at home. I hope my choice of words isn't too macabre for you.'

It wasn't. In fact, Cassandra found the ivy-clad Highgate scenery quite evocative. Sinuous paths climbed and descended the grounds that had been taken over by the greenery, manicured and groomed just enough not to seem derelict. At some places, the roots of the trees poked out from the ground and held to the flat headstones like crooked fingers to a handful of cards, playing a game against death that no one had ever won.

CHAPTER 5

In the Superintendent's House

Since Cassandra had been invited to stay in the superintendent's house for as long as the investigation would last, she arrived later the same day with her humble belongings packed into just one tapestry bag, the one with which she had fled her home many years ago.

No sooner had she put her foot on the first step of the stairs leading up to the superintendent's house when the door opened, and a woman fluttered out of the house. Chubby and energetic, with a youthful wreath of blonde curls around her face, she looked quite young, but wrinkles in the corners of her eyes gave away her maturity.

'Miss Ayers!' the woman of indefinite age exclaimed with the excitement of a girl, grabbing Cassandra's hand. 'I'm so thrilled to meet you. A lady detective. Haven't seen an investigation in my life.'

'Doris, let our guest be.' Mr Redlaw stepped out of the house and immediately took Cassandra's bag. 'Miss Ayers, this is my wife, Doris.'

'How do you do, Mrs Redlaw,' Cassandra said, shaking hands with her.

'Just Doris, please. May I call you Cassie?'

Cassandra opened her mouth to answer, but Mrs Redlaw wasn't expecting an answer as she went on:

'You are just as I imagined.'

'I wish my parents could say that.' Cassandra allowed herself a little irony.

Doris laughed, but looked unsure as to whether the statement was spoken in levity.

'Oh, please, come inside!' said Mr Redlaw, and invited Cassandra in with a gesture of his hand.

'Welcome to our home, Cassie,' Mrs Redlaw said.

'It is a lovely house.' Cassandra walked inside a cozy vestibule clad in dark wood. 'And your neighbours are very peaceful.' She nodded in the direction of the view the windows were overlooking.

Mrs Redlaw looked puzzled again. She followed Cassandra's gaze aimed at the cemetery, which could be seen from the windows of the vestibule, and then shifted her uncomprehending look to her husband.

'Miss Ayers is joking, darling,' he helped her out.

'Ah! You are a funny thing,' Mrs Redlaw said, and patted Cassandra on her back. 'We are quite used to living next to the cemetery. At first, I did find it a bit unnerving. You know, with all these dreadful stories...'

'Doris loves the folklore,' Mr Redlaw explained.

'Not all of it is folklore, my dearest,' his wife said. 'Did you know they found some of the graves empty after the outbreak of cholera in New York? Where did the bodies go? Some say it wasn't even cholera that took people's lives but...' she lowered her voice, 'vampires.'

'See what I have to put up with?' Mr Redlaw whispered to Cassandra in an amused tone.

'Believe me, Cassie, I am positively trembling when I think there's a wayward soul wandering among the graves,' the woman went on, disregarding her husband's ridicule.

A footman hurried to take Cassandra's baggage from Mr Redlaw and disappeared with it upstairs, almost bumping into a young woman who was descending the staircase.

'Ah, and here is our dear Miss Ellie Tesmond, my secretary,' Mr Redlaw said when the young woman had reached the bottom of the stairs and joined them.

'Good day,' Miss Tesmond said. She was a skinny and feeble-looking creature, tucked into a warm shawl. Her clothes were strikingly old-fashioned, even for someone uninterested in fashion trends like Cassandra. The round spectacles she wore made her eyes look small and beady.

'By the way, Miss Ayers, it was Miss Tesmond who saw the ghost,' Mrs Redlaw said excitedly. 'You should ask her. Or *interrogate* her. Is that the word you would use?'

Cassandra shook Miss Tesmond's bloodless hand.

'Yes. We will talk later if you don't mind, Miss Tesmond,' the detective said, engineering a friendly smile. Cassandra had learnt in practice that people were more eager to loosen their tongues with someone who smiled.

'Don't forget, Miss Ayers, that we expect you... ' Mr Redlaw began.

'...to dinner tonight,' Doris chimed in. 'Oh, I'm so thrilled.'

'All right, darling. Save some of your excitement for dinner, and allow Miss Tesmond to show Miss Ayers to her room,' said Mr Redlaw. 'We are late for another engagement. Will you please excuse us?'

'When we return, you will tell me everything about your investigations, my dear Cassie,' Mrs Redlaw chattered as her husband steered her away.

The two young women exchanged a look. The secretary could hardly stifle her smile.

'Mrs Redlaw is a good woman. A little restless, but good,' she said when they were climbing the stairs to the second storey of the house. 'She is like a mother figure to me. My own mother is long dead.'

'Do you have any other family?' Cassandra supported the conversation. A witness must feel the detective's genuine interest to be able to confide in them. Another great observation that came to her over the years.

'Only my brother. He's living in India now. But our relationships is, um, complicated.'

'Tell me about it,' Cassandra mumbled.

'You also have a brother?'

'Yes. And a complicated relationship. My mother is also long dead. As for the rest of my family, well, how can I put it nicely? We keep our distance. It's better for everyone.'

Miss Tesmond wrapped herself tighter into her shawl as if Cassandra's words suddenly made her feel cold.

'Families,' she said in an understanding tone.

Normally, Cassandra would not talk about her personal life, even to people she knew well, but working with witnesses, she would lower her guard, just a little, to let them know she was not talking to them from a position of power. People find it soothing to know the detective also has vulnerabilities. But, honestly, no one needs to know more about Cassandra's past than she is willing to share.

As they arrived at the end of the guest wing, Miss Tesmond opened one of the similar doors.

'This is your room,' she said. 'It's Mrs Redlaw's favourite.'

Cassandra stepped into the room that was so heavily loaded with floral ornaments and ruffs it made her feel quite ill. The wallpaper, drapes and bed sheets appeared to be under attack from millions of the tiniest crawling flowers and vines.

'Charming,' she said, peeling the gloves off her hands. A premonition told her that something much worse than flowery frenzy was creeping within these walls, and her premonition rarely let her down.

* * *

At teatime, Cassandra and Miss Tesmond were treated to a lemon sponge cake and loads of marzipan brought from Hungary by Mrs Redlaw's niece, a charming little thing who was going to marry the Duke of Beaufort's third son; mind you, it was a big secret just yet.

After tea, Mrs Redlaw took Cassandra and Miss Tesmond on a tour around the house and let them in on a dozen more family secrets, including the juiciest details of Prince Albert's, may he rest in peace, stay in their house with one of his lovers, whose name, of course, Mrs Redlaw did not have the right to divulge, except that her initials were *P.A.* With this, she meaningfully arched her eyebrows.

The woman had no shortage of sensational secrets, so Cassandra had to find a way to cork this breach, and she seized the opportunity to do so when they reached the secretary's office.

'Miss Tesmond, I remember Mr Redlaw said you were in charge of the registers.'

'Yes, I am.'

'I was wondering if you could provide me with the information about the two men whose graves have been defiled.'

'Oh, yes, by all means.' Miss Tesmond eagerly shook off the drowsiness she had been plunged into by Mrs Redlaw's endless cackling.

Stopped half-stride towards a piece of furniture related to yet another ravishing story, Mrs Redlaw made a gesture as if sealing her mouth, and went away on her toes, so as not to interfere with the *investigation*. Miss Tesmond chuckled and opened the door to her office, inviting Cassandra in.

The room, neat and strictly administrational, had in it a desk with an adjustable office chair at its side, and a bookcase holding even rows of registers inscribed in different handwritings through the years since Highgate Cemetery had opened in 1839.

While Miss Tesmond searched for the register the detective had requested, Cassandra observed the faceless study. One shelf seemed more personal than the others, decorated as it was with a statuette of a Harlequin of very fine work, but a little bit faded and chipped. His porcelain smirk made an eerie impression.

The shelf also held many volumes of poetry.

'You are fond of verse, Miss Tesmond?'

'It is my passion. Poetry offers another world, prettier than this abyss of hopelessness we live in.'

Cassandra turned her pensive gaze to the window overlooking the cemetery.

'Abyss of hopelessness,' she echoed.

'Do *you* take interest in poetry?' Miss Tesmond asked.

'Only in the darkest of it. *Here a pretty baby lies sung asleep with lullabies: pray be silent, and not stir the easy earth that covers her.*' Cassandra let the beauty of the verse waft in the air.

'Robert Herrick?'

'Yes. I find dark poetry more truthful than romantic. Death is very real, while love can be just an illusion.'

Little beady eyes of the secretary blinked at Cassandra as Miss Tesmond stood in front of her, holding to a little ladder.

'Well, you've certainly come to the right place to talk about death,' she said with a sad half-smile as she started climbing the steps. The secretary stretched to retrieve the register, dangling precariously from the ladder. She climbed down and put the register on the desk, wiping away the dust with a rag. 'This one has the information on burials in 1889. More than five hundred people were buried here that year. Strange, don't you think?'

Cassandra raised a questioning look at her.

'To us, these are only entries in a book, but there are personal tragedies attached to each and every one of them,' Miss Tesmond explained.

'I guess the insensibility to the sufferings of others helps us go on with our lives.'

'You could say that.'

Miss Tesmond mounted the ladder again to fetch the register for 1891.

Cassandra flipped through the pages of the 1889 register until she found the date 25 February 1889 and the name of Omer Ingleton, one of the deceased. Next of kin: son – Philip Ingleton. Address: 15 Arlington Street. The detective jotted the address down in her pocketbook.

Now, after a rapport had been established, it was time to ask the most important question.

'Tell me, Miss Tesmond, are you sure you saw a ghost?'

The secretary put the second volume on the desk. She averted her gaze.

'Don't get me wrong, Miss Ayers, I'm not some lunatic. I

consider myself a reasonable woman and a Christian. I don't gossip. You can ask Mr Redlaw.'

'We don't need to do that. I believe you.' Cassandra calmed her with a comforting smile. In fact, when was the last time she did not question everything that came out of people's mouths?

'Well, it's not easy to say,' the secretary went on, her hands fiddling with the sleeves of her dress, 'but I suffer from somnambulism.'

'You sleepwalk?'

'Mr and Mrs Redlaw know about it. They sympathize with my condition, and even let their doctor prescribe me medicine for better sleep. But it doesn't always work.'

'Don't worry, Miss Tesmond. I won't tell anyone about your condition if you want to keep it secret.'

'Thank you. People don't always understand. Some think it is dangerous. I know that some,' she added in a whisper, 'confine their family members to mental institutions. But I'm not crazy.'

'Believe me, I know a thing or two about mental institutions. Somnambulists are not insane. I've read about this. It is just a sleep disorder, nothing more.'

A sigh of relief escaped the secretary's chest. She briefly smiled.

'So what happened?' Cassandra asked.

Miss Tesmond's eyes became glazed as she stared into the void, recollecting.

'That night, I was sleepwalking again. Somehow, I got out of the house and walked to the cemetery. My feet usually take me down the routes I know well.'

'Do you often walk the cemetery during the day?'

'Yes. I sketch there.' She reached out for her leather-bound album for drawing, but suddenly changed her mind and withdrew her hand. 'It's nothing special, really. It's not that I have any talent. And then, when at the cemetery that night, a wail suddenly awakened me. I can almost assuredly report to you it was not a human voice. As soon as I realised where I was and what I'd heard, fear paralysed me because of all those rumours about the ghost. I looked around and found myself by a beautiful gravestone topped with a statue of an angel. There was no one around and no movement disturbed the darkness. But the wailing continued. It was such a sad sound, like a dog whimpering. And then I saw it. The ghost.'

'Can you describe it? Was it a man or woman? A child perhaps?'

'It was a vague figure hovering by the entrance to the Egyptian Avenue. It was insubstantial. If I had to guess, I'd say it was a young woman.'

"Insubstantial" was the word that Cassandra wrote down as Miss Tesmond kept describing it.

'Did you try to approach it?'

The woman shook her head, 'I couldn't. I was petrified. I was rooted to the spot. The figure stayed in place for a while, perhaps a minute, and then, suddenly, it just vanished.'

The secretary resurfaced from the depths of her memories, the terror in her eyes magnified by her thick spectacles.

'Please tell me you do not think me bereft of reason.'

'Bereft of reason? I think not.'

What the detective really thought was that someone was playing a dirty joke. But she kept her assumptions to herself. Instead, she wrote down the dry facts: the date when the encounter happened, the sound Miss Tesmond heard, the description of the site where she found herself in the night and the gravestone with the angel atop.

'What about the other witnesses?' she asked.

'You can ask Mr Ed Brockington, our former gardener. He resigned shortly after he saw the ghost.'

'Where can I find him?'

CHAPTER 6

Witnesses Who Saw Nothing

I f houses could talk, they would have a lot to say about their inhabitants.

Ed Brockington's house, devoured by greenery, was easy to overlook when walking down the street. Only its chimney stuck out of the green chaos, spitting a slender wisp of smoke into the grey sky.

Cassandra pushed open the wicket to the garden and walked down the narrow path. The house of brown brick at the end of it looked unwelcoming and clearly lacked the touch of a good master. Tiles were missing from the roof, spider webs carpeted the tools scattered near the shed, and the flowerbeds housed dry remains of what used to be begonias.

Long after Cassandra had knocked and just as she was about to turn away, a man's face peeked through the crack in the open door. His untidy hair and bristle completed the full picture of neglect.

Ed Brockington gazed at Cassandra with suspicion.

'Good day, Mr Brockington. My name is Cassandra Ayers. I'm here to ask you a couple of questions about your service at Highgate Cemetery.'

'What about it?' he asked in a tone far from friendly.

'May I come in?'

The man eyed Cassandra up and down before he stepped aside and let her enter.

Inside, everything was filthy, disordered and reeking of tobacco, though the main source of the smell was the owner of the property himself. The table was piled high with dirty mugs and plates, and there were food leftovers strewn across the scratched surface of the table.

Amidst all this mess, a neat and prettily arranged basket of food looked alien, sitting on the bench, almost certainly brought over by a caring woman, a mother or sister perhaps, since Ed Brockington was not married.

He stumped across his dwelling like a ruthless captain in his shabby pirate ship. Cassandra couldn't say for sure why he resembled a pirate – maybe because his face was so tanned and weather-beaten.

'So what is it you want to know, Missy?' the groundsman asked, throwing a filthy napkin onto the basket in an obvious attempt to conceal it from the intruder who was in that moment staring right at it. He flopped into a squashy armchair worn and shaped into a hollow imprint by several generations of his family's bottoms.

The detective looked around for a place to sit but decided to remain standing – there was nothing adequately clean.

'How long had you worked at Highgate Cemetery?' she asked.

'About a year. Maybe more,' Brockington shrugged his shoulders.

'How long ago did you first encounter the supernatural?'

'Why? Are you a journalist or somefing?'

'No. Mr Redlaw has hired me to investigate the case of some desecrated graves.'

Ed Brockington gave a sharp chuckle as he took out his pipe. An inner tremble – a sign of her opium addiction – rushed down Cassandra's limbs as she watched his deft fingers fill the pipe.

'A woman detective! My word, vis country is going down'ill.' Ed Brockington rasped and put the mouthpiece into the corner of his mouth.

Cassandra sighed, unimpressed. If only she got paid a penny every time people made jokes about it, she would be rich as a caliph.

'Your co-operation would help Mr Redlaw. He praised your work. I'm sure it was hard for him to lose such a skilled gardener.' A usual soothing smile appeared on Cassandra's lips. She knew men just like Brockington: they would easily side with you in return for a good, fat compliment to balm their pride.

The man shook the flame off the tip of the match and flicked it into the cold fireplace. 'If it 'elps Mr Redlaw. A capital chap 'e is. Capital. I was sorry to leave 'is employ. 'Ow long ago you ask?' He pulled on the pipe several times, thinking, his lips smacking. 'Can't say for sure. It was still cold. That's what I remember. Early spring. There was a bit of snow 'ere and there when I worked on the cemetery grounds that day.'

'And what exactly did you see?' Cassandra asked.

'Oh, prepare yourself for a bit of a shocker. Maybe better sit, lassie.'

'Don't worry. I've got a strong stomach.' She remained standing.

'Suit yourself. So that was a late evening when it all 'appened. I returned to check on 'Armon, a boy who worked with me at the cemetery. I 'eard a sound, a weeping. Thought it was just some woman. You know, sometimes them poor souls come to visit a grave and lose track of time. I followed the sound. Wanted to see 'er off. But what I saw wasn't a lass.' He stopped for a dramatic, suspenseful moment. 'It was a vague figure.'

'Where was it?'

'By the Egyptian Avenue. Never liked that place.'

'Can you describe it?'

'Well... tall... six feet, not less. It 'overed over the ground. Its body was see-through. And the colour... I'd call it milky or pale.'

The detective's pencil scratched loudly against the surface of the page as she wrote it all down, summarizing it with a note that read, "Classic description of a ghost – could have picked it up from someone."

'Mm-hmm,' she mumbled. 'Did you see any particular features? Eyes, hair, the shape of its nose?'

'Special features,' the man exclaimed grumpily. 'I saw a bloody ghost. I didn't pay no attention to its nose, Missy.'

'You make an impression of a reasonable and attentive man,' Cassandra sugared it again. 'I'm sure you noticed something special.'

The man chewed on the tobacco for a while, retrieving the bits of his memories about that night.

'Its face was vague. I'd call it insubstantitive.'

'Insubstantial?' the detective corrected him.

'Maybe. I went to no school. You know better.'

Jotting the word down, Cassandra made a note that Miss Tesmond used the same word to describe the ghost.

'Did you talk about the encounter with anyone from the cemetery?'

'No. I resigned that very night. After I found 'Armon 'iding in the crypt, trembling and unable to utter a word, we both resigned that very evening.'

'And you talked to no one about what you'd seen?'

'Like I told ya, no. No.'

'You didn't describe it to Mr Redlaw, his wife or secretary?'

Ed Brockington stubbornly shook his head of unkempt hair.

'I told Mr Redlaw I was sorry, that's what. And left.'

'Mm-hmm.'

'Believe me, Missy, I'm not a man of superstitions, but vat fing scared the 'ell out of me.'

And yet, the use of the same words in describing the ghost made Cassandra think the witnesses' experience could have been prompted by the prior conversations about the ghosts. Could she accept their words as truthful? Could she rely on the recounting of events from people who had heard about the ghost and what it looked like, and had obviously premeditated a description clouded by the opinion of others?

Leaving Mr Brockington's home and walking again through the garden, the sleuth could not get rid of the feeling that something was off. She stopped at the wicket and studied the place with a careful gaze that never missed a thing. The wilted begonias and untamed bushes pointed out what had been nagging her somewhere at the back of her mind: isn't it weird that such a good gardener did not maintain the good looks of his own garden?

* * *

Harmon Dilworth had the expression of a simpleton. He sat across from Cassandra, fidgeting nervously, while his rosy-cheeked mother poured a cup of tea for their guest.

'I was cutting some vegetation. You know...' Harmon said and rubbed one of his floppy ears.

'You were with Mr Brockington,' his mother prompted him.

'Yes. Yes, I was!'

'It's not like he is making it up. Mr Brockington can prove it,' Harmon's mother said hastily.

'It's all right, Mrs Dilworth. I believe Harmon.' Cassandra smiled reassuringly at the boy. He simpered back at her and stole a sheepish glance at his mother.

'Good. My son never lies, Miss Ayers. Never. We are a respectable family.'

She smoothed her son's hair as if he were just a toddler, not a grown man. The two of them made a rather comical pair. Mrs Dilworth, short and plump, in her bright florid apron and a head of curly hair of the most outrageous shade of red, resembled a gnome from a fairy tale. In stark contrast, Harmon was the lanky owner of hair that hardly boasted any colour at all. In the absence of a better word, Cassandra would call his hair mousy.

Although everything was decently maintained in their tiny slice of a home, tucked in the least favoured part of the city, their poverty was obvious. From what Cassandra learnt, Mrs Dilworth sewed and patched some linen for her middle-class clients. As for Harmon, he now worked at a gas station where he shovelled coal into a furnace sixteen hours a day. His hands were covered in blisters, and the soot on his knuckles appeared as though it was there to stay. The detective gathered it was a painful loss for Harmon when he resigned from his position at the cemetery.

'Those 'ands.' Mrs Dilworth swatted at her son's hands with a towel.

'What was it you were saying, Harmon?' The detective tried to channel the boy's attention towards the conversation again.

He rubbed his sooty palms against his knees.

'I was walking frough the Egyptian Avenue with me wheelbarrow. I 'eard vis sound.' He whimpered like a distressed dog. 'I got very scared, and I couldn't move. And ven it grabbed me 'and.' Harmon extended his skinny limb to show where the ghost touched him. 'I dropped me tools and ran away.'

'So you saw nothing? But you heard sounds and felt a touch?' Cassandra asked.

'No, Miss. I mean yes, Miss. Mr Brockington can prove it, Miss. 'E found me in the crypt. Only God knows what could've 'appened to me but for Mr Brockington.'

'Vat man really took care of me boy,' Mrs Dilworth chimed in.

The detective wrote it all down.

'I didn't see it. I didn't,' Harmon shook his head, disappointed at himself.

Cassandra visited seven houses that day, where other gardeners who'd resigned from Highgate Cemetery lived. They repeated the same story: no one had seen the ghost, but they had all heard it or smelled it, even felt it.

'You only heard the ghost?' Cassandra clarified when speaking to one of them.

'Yes. I haven't seen it. But Mr Brockington has. He described it in detail.'

'I bet he did,' she said, suspicion spawning in her head.

CHAPTER 7

Beyond What Man's Eyes Can See

An evening in the company of people she barely knew was something Cassandra would gladly avoid, but with Mrs Redlaw too eager to have the detective among her guests, there was no chance of escaping, even if Cassandra were on her death bed. Small talk and parlour games had never been her strong suits. Since she had fled Caxton Hall a few years ago and stopped frequenting dinners and balls, her social skills had become even rustier.

Perspiring in her elegant evening dress more than she would care to admit, Cassandra was walking down the stairs when she saw a man entering the vestibule. He saw her, too, and his lips curled into a smile while he was passing his hat and coat to the butler. No doubt, he was trying to come up with something smug. It was Valentine Duvar himself.

'What are you doing here?' the detective asked, reaching the foot of the stairs.

'A crank like myself, as you dubbed me, couldn't resist a chance to sniff around a bit.'

'Are you always so amused by what people say about you?'

'Well, I can't allow them to get to me, so I prefer to take everything lightly.'

'A rare privilege.'

'Not exactly a privilege; rather, a deliberate choice.'

'As you wish.'

Valentine caught up with her as she headed for the drawing room, the drone of guests' voices already audible.

'I played the card of my family's high social standing to get an invitation to this evening. I hope you don't mind,' he went on teasing.

'I couldn't care less.'

As soon as the footman opened the door to the drawing room for the two of them, Cassandra understood that Valentine Duvar was not her worst nightmare for the evening. Standing by the fireplace, twitching his silly handlebar moustache, was Captain Drummond himself. Lavinia, his wife and Cassandra's old friend, was gently leaning on her husband's arm. That was the moment when her death bed seemed a rather pleasant alternative.

'Here she is, our dearest guest.' Mrs Redlaw immediately hooked her arm through Cassandra's and steered her around the room with the intention of introducing her to everyone present. 'Reverend Gummidge, this is Miss Cassandra Ayers.'

'Yes. We've already met.' The reverend's smile resembled a wincing expression caused by toothache.

'When did that happen?' Mrs Redlaw asked.

'We met when I'd just arrived at the cemetery,' the detective explained. 'Reverend Gummidge was in a great hurry, though.'

The old man winced even more at this gibe.

'Let me, then, introduce you to Captain Drummond,' the mistress of the house said, pulling at Cassandra's hand and delivering her front and centre to a man attired in a scarlet military tunic. His chest was wide enough for a host of decorations, but it was adorned by none. As the handlebar moustache turned in her direction, Cassandra and Drummond exchanged cold stares.

'Darling, you are not attentive,' Mr Redlaw said gently to his wife. 'Miss Ayers and our Lavinia are old school friends. Of course, Miss Ayers and Captain Drummond know each other. I'm sure you were at their wedding, too,' he addressed Cassandra.

That was an opportunity to have a dig at Drummond and the

detective gladly used it. 'Actually, I wasn't invited.'

'I say.' The superintendent was taken aback. 'Why is that?'

The couple looked away. Cassandra would give her right hand to hear the answer, but she decided it was wiser to come to their rescue.

'I'm afraid other engagements kept me busy anyway,' she said.

Mr Redlaw did not seem satisfied with the answer and looked disapprovingly at his niece as if she had just informed him that she was going to become a prostitute. Luckily, his wife edged in on the conversation.

'I am positively disappointed. Everybody already knows everybody. The introduction of my most unusual guest, a lady detective, was supposed to be the sensation of this evening.'

'Some sensation,' Drummond said into his glass of wine, so that no one but Cassandra and Lavinia could hear what he had mumbled.

'I am no sensation, but I'll be glad to be introduced, too.' Valentine stepped closer to their circle.

'I do apologize.' Mrs Redlaw came to her senses. 'Allow me to introduce Mr Valentine Duvar.'

'Duvar,' Drummond repeated the name. 'Duvar. Sounds familiar.'

'Maybe because I've made a name in photography.'

The captain's face lit up. 'Isn't Lord Salisbury your father?' The career of a photographer did not fascinate him in the least, compared to the prospect of rubbing shoulders with the Salisburys.

Valentine's never-fading smile flinched just a little, to Cassandra's great amusement: she was glad to witness the jostling between Drummond's snobbery and Duvar's cheekiness.

'Yes. He is my father.'

'How splendid. Last year, His Lordship invited some of the lucky officers, including me, to his family house in Dorset,' Drummond said with a happy twinkle in his eye. 'Such a grand mansion.'

'After that visit, William talked for days on end about the hunting on His Lordship's grounds,' Lavinia confirmed with the most genuine smile.

'Did he?' Valentine sipped his wine, failing to disguise his utmost disinterest.

Drummond began to say something about the highlights of that day in Dorset, but was interrupted immediately by Valentine, 'You can save your stories, Captain. I'm not a big fan of hunting.'

'That's a shame. Living in such a great mansion must be...'

'I don't often go there. Being the younger son, I was supposed to become a military man or a clergyman, but I chose the career of a photographer. Apparently, that's not good enough to tread the Persian carpets in the Salisbury home,' Valentine said through a smile, though Cassandra caught a note of sadness in Valentine's voice. She peeked at him over the rim of her glass and couldn't help but see him differently now.

Such frankness, frowned upon in the refined living rooms of high society, hushed everyone. They all took a moment to sip from their aperitif. Only now did the detective notice Miss Tesmond in her modest gown, standing by the grand piano. She seemed far away in her thoughts and absolutely not interested in either Drummond's exalted hunting memories or Duvar's family squabbles.

* * *

At dinner, Mr and Mrs Redlaw each sat at opposite ends of the dining table, maneuvering the conversation between their guests, so that every lamb chop was garnished with a big portion of small talk. Cassandra anticipated indigestion. She sat to the right of the mistress of the house; her company on the other side was Valentine.

For some time, the conversation at the table was dominated by news and topics about which the detective had nothing to say.

'Such a tragedy. She was only sixteen,' Mr Redlaw said.

There was never a lack of thrilling tragedies to discuss at

the table of the cemetery superintendent. Over and over the talk revolved around those who deceased too early, or too brutally; those whose funerals were attended by droves of mourners, and those who were scandalously abandoned; those who were buried in inlaid oak coffins, and those who were laid under plain headstones which still left their families in debt; people from all walks of life who were interesting subjects for a conversation through one fact only – they were dead.

'We sent them a nice big wreath of lilies,' Mrs Redlaw added.

She looked at the guests to see their appreciation. Lavinia supported Mrs Redlaw's thoughtfulness with a gentle, womanly smile. Drummond nodded to the mistress of the house, acknowledging her Christian kindness.

'Nothing makes a better gossip than somebody's untimely death,' Valentine whispered to Cassandra. She cracked a smile while stirring the soup in her plate. Since childhood, she had suffered from the absence of appetite – the reason why she was so thin. Dr Bentzel, whom she would like to forget, said it was caused by her nervous state. She scooped a bit of soup, just on the tip of the spoon, and took a tiny sip.

'God works in mysterious ways,' Reverend Gummidge opined on the death of the sixteen-year-old girl they had been speaking about. 'This turtle soup is capital.'

Cassandra stopped with her spoon halfway to her mouth, just for a second, to digest the Reverend's indifferent remark about the girl, as he wolfed down his soup. She placed her spoon back into the soup plate, her appetite completely lost.

Mrs Redlaw's eyes darted around the table in search of a new topic to cut the building tension. She stole a curious look at the detective, the most peculiar guest she had ever received. Surely her guests would be entertained with the fascinating stories of the cases she must have solved.

'Miss Ayers,' she began. 'Mr Redlaw tells me you earn your own living.'

Everyone stared at Cassandra with such intensity it was as though all of them had been waiting for this moment and this moment alone, when the conversation would find and latch on to her.

'I must, since there's no one to do it in my stead,' she finally replied.

'How *extraordinary*,' Drummond said stressing the last word, obviously meaning something else.

'Miss Ayers is representative of a new era, Drummond,' Mr Redlaw said, raising his glass in an appreciative gesture. 'I say, I find it rather exciting to be sitting at a table with a woman detective.'

'I would rather see the world unchanged, where men and women have their place pleasing to God,' the Reverend opined. He finished his soup and wiped his lips with a napkin.

'I quite agree,' Drummond said.

The Reverend's Biblical reference cut through the air like a whip, leaving it charged, while everyone took some time to reflect on his little speech. After all, the clergymen's words were to be contemplated in respectful silence, not contradicted. But Cassandra could not leave it; otherwise, she would burst at the seams with corked-up annoyance.

'And in your unchanged world, Reverend, we would still burn witches?' she asked, watching as he was served the lamb.

'Touché,' Valentine whispered to no one in particular, except his own plate.

Mr Redlaw stifled a smile. Gummidge, sitting next to him, finally stopped eating and looked directly at the detective, unblinking.

'I understand your irony, Miss Ayers, but...' he started.

'I presume, you've seen many otherworldly things during your most intriguing career, Miss Ayers?' Mrs Redlaw interrupted the clergyman, saving everyone from another pious speech.

'Only if what you call *otherworldly* means packs of conmen, dirty schemes, thugs pretending to be someone's deceased relatives and women accused of witchcraft because they picked some herbs at night,' Cassandra said.

Judging from the reaction, they had all expected to hear something different. The detective was used to this. People always asked her about the witches and werewolves she destroyed, and almost always she was met with disenchanted faces when she told them she had actually never seen anything more supernatural than man's evil eye and emotional vampirism.

'But there must be something to this world beyond what man's eyes can see.' Miss Tesmond sounded disappointed. 'Otherwise, our existence would be a journey with a sad and lonely end.'

The sad and lonely end in the spiritless void of existence was what scared Cassandra in the night. Yet, if there was evidence to the contrary, she had not been lucky enough to find it, and she was about to say exactly that when a hunch came over her and silenced her. It was prompted by the secretary's remark about what man's eye can't see. Cassandra observed Miss Tesmond's glasses while the suspicion was forming. She would have to check one thing.

'There is something greater to our existence. Our faith in God.' Reverend Gummidge used the pause to interject. 'And I am glad you, Miss Ayers, are fighting to demystify all those pagan old wives' tales and ungodly superstitions.'

'With all due respect, Reverend, I do not say I don't believe in the supernatural. I only say I can't believe in something until I have seen it myself,' the detective stated firmly. 'The same as I have never seen a clergyman turn wine into blood and bread into flesh.'

There was a ripple of uneasiness around the table. A convulsion of a concealed smile touched Mr Redlaw's face. The conversation was lost until the servants brought in the dessert. Mrs Redlaw sighed happily and started explaining how she was about to mistakenly use the washing powder instead of vanilla for the old English trifle she herself had prepared for the guests.

'But for my dear Lucy, my maid, I would have made a terrible mistake. My reputation of a good mistress of this house would have been ruined, for everyone knows I make all the desserts myself.'

'I always pamper my dear William with something sweet, too. When not occupied with many other housekeeping chores,' Lavinia said, gently caressing her husband's hand.

Cassandra fiercely scooped a chunk of dessert, the spoon screeching against the plate. Before she could think better of it, she made a remark, 'A good wife must know so many things: how to bake cakes, embroider napkins, make concoctions and treat runny noses, let alone her obligation to commit her entire life to pleasing her husband. Or the word *woman* will be but half-deserved.'

'Indeed! How can one person possibly know all these things?' Valentine exclaimed.

Flustered at the poorly veiled ridicule, Lavinia stared at her trifle, having suddenly lost her appetite.

'You despise women, Miss Ayers?' Drummond asked.

'I don't appreciate what men have done to them.'

'There must have been something disturbing in your past, Miss Ayers, something that makes you think this way about the sacred marital institution,' he spoke to her across the table.

'I've seen many marriages. Few were sacred.'

'This is extraordinary,' the captain smirked – he'd expected this.

The conversation was becoming more and more unpleasant, and Cassandra reproved herself for sharing her unpopular opinions she knew would trigger a bitter debate.

'What happened to you to make you think this way?' The captain was not willing to let it go.

'Mrs Redlaw, my compliments to you.' She tried to compensate for her own mistake. 'This trifle is delicious.'

'Thank you, my dear. I can give you my recipe if...'

'Indulge us, Cassie. Since you're so chatty today,' Lavinia edged in, 'tell us one of your fascinating life stories.'

Cassandra stared at her, trying to shush her friend. Everyone waited with bated breaths.

'Here is one of my favourites,' Lavinia went on, filling her mouth with a generous bite of trifle. 'Cassie used to tell me that after her mother's death, she started hearing voices in her head. Which is why she was treated for insanity in the asylum.'

Everyone inhaled sharply and froze, expecting and dreading the continuation. The cutlery stopped clinking, and the trifle was left without attention, smeared over the plates. Lavinia wiped the corners of her mouth as she swallowed the dessert.

'But as I can see, some things cannot be cured,' she concluded.

It felt as if a volcano had erupted inside Cassandra's chest. Heat scorched her throat and made her face burn. She sat, numb, staring at Lavinia, her lifelong friend.

'Good Lord!' Reverend Gummidge crossed himself.

Eventually, Cassandra found her tongue saying, 'Who didn't make up stories when young?'

The clock tick-tocked its presence into the silence of the dining room. A long and awkward pause gave everyone time for a big drink. Mrs Redlaw forced a smile above the ruins of what was supposed to be a charming evening.

'Does anyone care for a game of Preferans?' she asked.

* * *

The evening dragged on and on. One game of Preferans turned into another. When Cassandra finally returned to her room, she was completely exhausted. She sat on the edge of her bed, slumping under the burden of everything she had heard, but mostly under the weight of everything she had said. Why couldn't she just keep her mouth shut? Why did she always need to share her opinions? It never ended well.

When somebody knocked on her door, Cassandra didn't respond. She sat quietly on her bed, her hands locked around the box containing her outfit for smoking opium, waiting for the uninvited caller to leave. But they didn't. Cassandra watched in anticipation as the door handle turned. She quickly tucked her opium box under her pillow just as Lavinia entered, hands hidden in a muff, a giant hat with a cascade of feathers perfectly positioned on her head. In fact, the hat was so big, Cassandra imagined it breaking her friend's slender neck. The elegantly dressed woman stepped into the room with the merciless expression of an executioner.

'I have never been so humiliated in my entire life,' her voice trembled with anger. 'I hope you're proud of yourself.'

'I'm sorry I offended you.'

Lavinia exhaled the remains of her anger and turned to the door to leave, rather unsatisfied and tired.

'Can I ask you for one thing?' Cassandra said before her friend had stepped out of the room.

The head bearing the huge plateau of feathers turned back to her; the expression on her face was incredulous.

'I don't know if you are in a position to be asking anything of me.' A long pause followed. 'What is it?'

'Those things you said at the table about my childhood... I didn't want people to know about them. Can I trust you to never tell them to anyone else, ever again?'

The answer was a brief nod of the head in the huge hat.

'Those were distasteful tales, anyway.'

'Of course, they were.' A sad smile touched Cassandra's lips.

The instant the door closed behind Lavinia, Cassandra buried her face in her palms. Her body began to tremble; stifled sobs stuck in her throat and choked her.

The terrible images of her childhood flashed in rapid succession through her memory. They were distasteful, indeed, but not untrue.

CHAPTER 8

The Ingletons and The Rickets

The night terrors invaded her subconscious once again. Shattered memories that had no explanation inundated her dreams. She was thirteen, trying to get out of the coffin whose lid was locked tight. Enveloped in the overpowering smell of lilies, Cassie was suffocating. It seemed she was going to die in the tiny confinement of the coffin, with no air to breathe. But then she heard an inhuman growl. It was outside the coffin, approaching. Something powerful tore open the lid. Cassie saw it hovering over her, but the image in her memory was so blurred she couldn't see clearly what it was. Whatever she saw, it was so terrifying, she fainted.

Cassandra sat up in her bed in a cold sweat and spent a few minutes calming down her racing heart, trying to understand if what she had just seen in the nightmare had actually ever happened. But all these fragmented pieces that surfaced in her subconscious every night were too scary to be true. She could not possibly have witnessed all the terrifying things that haunted her in the nights. The fall from the Family Gallery at Caxton Hall must have badly damaged her head, taking away most of the memories of her childhood. And all these terrors must be just the games of her mind still trying to piece together what was left from her past experiences.

The light was struggling to break into the room through a crack in the heavy velvet draping hanging over the window. The sun was poking its finger right into her eye, telling Cassandra to rise and start a new page of her existence. She hated mornings because of the premonition of all the dreadful things that might happen, and she dreaded nights for the anticipation of the terrors she was about to see. She had to break the vicious circle but did not know how.

Rubbing the sleepiness from her face, Cassandra heard footsteps in the hallway approaching her room. The detective flung off the throw and sprinted across the room to stash the smoking set in her travelling bag, just as the maid arrived and let herself in after a quiet knock.

'Good morning,' the young woman said, traversing the room and opening the curtains.

'Is it, though?' Cassandra disappeared behind the screen and splashed some water onto her face, then soaked the towel in the water and started washing her body.

A long pause followed her remark. Normally, the servants were trained to not respond to the masters' sarcasm. But not this one, obviously, because she said, with a detectible smile in her voice, 'We heard you put up a fight yesterday.'

By *we* she meant the servants, of course.

'I'm not sure that qualifies as a fight,' the detective answered, applying soap on her body.

'I can't give my piece of mind to the masters, but I'm glad there's someone who dares tell them the truth.'

Cassandra stepped out from behind the screen, giving the maid a questioning look.

'All the servants are on your side, if you want to know,' the young and daring woman said, raising her chin.

'And what side is that?'

'The side that craves change. For women, children, poor and all the neglected.'

Deep down Cassandra was pleased to hear that her outrageous behaviour the day before was not condemned by at least one person. But she was not at all sure she could take the credit for trying to change the world. The only thing she wanted to achieve was to point out how preposterous were the views held by Captain Drummond and Reverend Gummidge.

'Here.' The maid took out a folded piece of paper from the pocket in her apron and extended it to the detective. Cassandra unfolded it. It was a call to attend a gathering where a certain Emmeline Pankhurst was going to talk about the necessary changes society had to undertake to improve the position of women. The words that stood out prominently in the manifesto were *education, equality, right to vote.*

'I'm afraid I'm not that type of person whom they are looking for.' Cassandra shook her head and tried to return the invitation to the maid.

'Don't worry, madam. Not one of us is that type of person.' She refused to take back the paper and instead picked up Cassandra's gown and helped the guest into it.

As the maid buttoned up and laced her corset, the detective was still looking at the printed call. The event was to happen on October 13, 1900, in five days. Skeptical of any people's gatherings for a cause, she sighed and made a deal with herself: if she solved the Highgate case by that time, she would go to the rally.

On her way downstairs for breakfast, Cassandra mentally prepared a speech, an apology she felt she owed Mr and Mrs Redlaw for her scandalous behaviour the evening before, and, she had decided, an apology such as this was best delivered to her hosts right before breakfast.

Her expertise in apologizing was extensive, for people always expected her to feel sorry for being what she was. The constant practice of apologizing to her father, stepmother, brother and numerous relatives and family friends made her expectedly good at it.

Mr Redlaw, his wife and Miss Tesmond were already at the table when Cassandra entered the dining room.

'Good morning, Miss Ayers.' The secretary was first to notice her.

'I must apologize for yesterday,' the detective said before she could join the three of them at the table.

Mrs Redlaw, her head in a cap, the form of which resembled a wilted bellflower bud, turned to Cassandra.

'Nonsense,' the woman exclaimed. She sprang to her feet, took the guest by her hand, and brought her to the table.

'We are not angry with you, Miss Ayers.' Mr Redlaw folded his newspaper.

'But I'd say a word or two to Captain Drummond.' The mistress of the house started putting toasts, butter and jam closer to Cassandra. 'The man doesn't have the slightest notion of what a civilized conversation is. An insufferable man. And Lavinia! What was she thinking, saying things like that?'

She bulged her eyes at her husband as if it was his fault his niece was such a piece of work.

'I'm afraid I provoked them with my sarcastic remarks,' Cassandra admitted.

'Then, they must learn how to handle a more subtle exchange of gibes. The conversation yesterday showed quite clearly that they can't,' Mr Redlaw concluded. 'They will hear about it from me.'

'Please, I don't want to bring any tension to your relationship with Lavinia. I couldn't bear to think I caused a conflict between you,' the detective said. 'You are the only father she's ever had.'

The words took a soothing effect on the superintendent, and he sighed.

'All right, then. Let's all forget about it, shall we?' was his solution.

They all accepted this with an eager nod, smiled at each other and got down to their breakfast. The meal passed to the pleasant accompaniment of Mrs Redlaw's cheerful chirruping, which Cassandra was strangely delighted to hear again.

* * *

After breakfast, the hansom cab took the detective to 15 Arlington Street, where, according to the register, Omer Ingleton's son, Philip, lived. She knocked on the door of an elegant and impeccably white townhouse.

The big heavy door opened to reveal an equally impeccable-looking butler who asked of the visitor what her business was with the master. The sides of his white hair were swept up and over to cover the baldness on his head.

'I'm here to see Mr Ingleton.'

'And you are?'

'Cassandra Ayers.'

'Is Mr Ingleton expecting you?'

'I don't think so.'

'Then, I'm afraid –'

The butler was already closing the door but couldn't with Cassandra's foot planted firmly in its way.

'I just need to talk to him about his father's grave,' she said, squeezing through the opening and slipping into the hall.

For a moment, the butler was so astounded by Cassandra's invasion, he could not speak. He might have said something, had his ability to speak not continued to elude him, but, when he took in the visitor's dress, her decadent walking stick, sunglasses and man's-style bowler hat, all he could manage was the involuntary tightening of his face into a mask etched with disapproval.

'I've been hired by the superintendent of the cemetery to find the people who are responsible for the desecration of Mr Omer Ingleton's grave. I really must speak with his son,' she said and extended her calling card.

The butler looked skeptically at the card that introduced Cassandra as a private detective. Tight-lipped, he pulled a ribbon on the wall to call a footman. A servant's door, disguised as a wooden panel on the wall, suddenly opened and through it appeared a young boy who scurried towards them, with the innocence of a first moustache on his upper lip.

'William, stay here with Miss Ayers while I'm gone,' the butler said, and disappeared into the adjacent sitting room.

'Yes, Mr Ogbourne.'

Cassandra stayed in the hall under the supervision of the young footman, while the butler was away speaking to his master. The boy avoided her gaze and sighed at times to politely fill the awkward silence with at least some sounds of their presence.

'Mr Ingleton and Mrs Carstone are ready to receive you,' the butler announced as he returned and held the door for her to enter the sitting room.

Cassandra entered the richly furnished room, overly adorned with little naked Cupid butts. Philip Ingleton, a man of around forty, stood by the fireplace with the airs of Napoleon posing for a portrait. His sister, Luisa Carstone, sat in an armchair with the countenance of a queen who had suddenly smelled shit. There was no need to be a detective to instantly recognize the type of people they were: *nouveau riche* with no origin, but with a fortune sufficient to buy the appearance of such.

'Investigating the case? You?' Luisa asked, the stench of shit crawling deeper into her nostrils. 'Fiddle-de-dee!'

Cassandra ignored the remark.

'I have just a couple of questions. It won't take long.'

'This is a ridiculous idea. What can you possibly investigate?'

Chuckles and snorts.

'You'd do a great favour to Mr Redlaw and...' she hated herself for saying this, 'and to Lord Salisbury's son, who takes a great interest in the investigation.'

'Oh.' The two *nouveau riche* appreciated the name-dropping tactics, and their expressions showed they were now prepared to listen.

'Do you know anyone who would want to do damage to your father's grave? Did he have enemies?' she went on.

'Our father was an honourable man,' Philip retorted.

'Honourable people have enemies, like anyone else,' the detective said.

While thinking, he sucked at a piece of something between his teeth. The noise of his exceptional effort to dislodge whatever it was finally ceased, but he wasted no time in substituting one bad behaviour with another when he proceeded to pick between his teeth with the fingernail of his baby finger. As she watched Philip retrieve the crumb and flick it from a fingernail clearly grown for the purpose of snorting cocaine, it reinforced her opinion that money cannot buy couth. Wherever it landed was anybody's guess, but it was certainly somewhere on the expensive Persian rug.

'I assure you, *detective*, we don't have enemies. And now, if you will excuse us,' Philip said, stepping forward with his hand extended in an effort to drive her out of the room.

'I haven't finished yet,' she said as she took out her pocketbook.

'Well, you have a nerve,' Luisa cackled, and began waving her fan more vigorously.

Philip opened his mouth to further protest, but closed it again.

'Has anything unusual happened recently?' Cassandra asked, her pencil poised, as Philip slinked into an armchair next to his sister.

'No,' Luisa said.

'Not that I can think of.' Philip removed a fleck of dust from his knee.

Cassandra opened her notebook and showed them the page where she had copied the symbol from the headstone.

'Can you tell me what it means?' she asked.

They both craned over the notebook. A nervous tick pinched one side of Philip's face as he saw the sketch. Luisa suddenly began to smooth the wrinkles on her gown, awkwardly averting her eyes.

'This is what our father wanted us to engrave on his tombstone,' Philip explained.

'And you don't have the slightest idea what it might be?'

'He was demented, the man. You happy, you little snoop?' Luisa blurted out. 'Why are you permitting this woman to invade our home like this?' she hissed at her brother under her breath.

'That's enough,' Philip said. 'I am ordering you to leave.'

* * *

Luisa peeked out of the window to make sure Cassandra had crossed the street and walked away before turning to her brother and sharing a long, silent exchange.

'This one is a real trackhound,' the woman said. 'She'll be stalking us until she finds out everything. We can't let this happen.'

Philip nodded and left the room with a look of purpose on his face. He then returned with a stack of letters and approached the fireplace, where the unsuspecting little fire cuddled to a log. The man unfolded one of the letters as if to remind himself of the content. The sloppy and unnaturally big handwriting read, *Give us what is ours. Or you will pay dearly.*

'What are you waiting for?' Luisa croaked from the depth of the room, pacing restlessly.

One by one Philip tossed the letters into the fire and watched the tiny flame grow into a bright blaze that hungrily devoured their secret.

* * *

Another cab took Cassandra to Russell Square. Houses here were not as freshly painted as on Arlington Street, and some places reeked of piss. As she looked for the address written on a patch of paper in her hand, the cold wind pulled at Cassandra's skirt like an insistent lover who just would not take no for an answer.

Here it was, the house where Nathan Ricket's family lived, according to the cemetery register. The building made a gloomy impression, with tapestries of mould hanging on its walls, and crumbled ledges under windows that knew cleaner days.

Holding on to her little bowler hat with her hand on top of her head, Cassandra trudged up the worn steps leading to the entrance of the house. Her rigid leg was throbbing.

An old woman with dark shadows under her eyes answered the door.

'Good morning,' the detective said. 'My name is Cassandra Ayers. I am looking for the Ricket family. Do they still live here?'

Instead of the answer, the woman eyed the visitor up and down, and on seeing her reasonably expensive attire, let her in. She introduced herself as the landlady of this piss-soaked property and escorted Cassandra up to the second floor, where there were rooms rented by the Rickets.

'What is your business with them? Have they done anything wrong?' the landlady asked suspiciously, panting on the steep ascent. 'They seem like such good tenants.'

'No. They did nothing wrong. I am here to ask them a couple of questions. Maybe they can help me locate someone.'

The two women arrived at a door that was in desperate need of a fresh coat of paint: dry, cracked and peeling paint was flaking in big sheets off the door, making it difficult for the landlady to find a spot where to knock.

A neatly dressed woman of Cassandra's age peeked through the narrow opening in the doorway.

'Margie Ricket?' the detective asked.

'Yes.' The young woman sounded wary.

'My name's Cassandra Ayers. I'm investigating the desecration of some graves at Highgate Cemetery, one of which was your father's. I'm trying to determine who was responsible for that.'

'Oh!' Margie exclaimed, suddenly relieved, like a person who had already seen most unwelcome visitors on her threshold and now was glad it wasn't one of them, but then she frowned and added, 'What a dreadful business. Please, come in, Miss Ayers.'

The landlady lingered a bit just beyond the door, expecting to overhear some more curious details, but Margie shut the door in her face.

'I thought you were one of the usurers,' Margie said, explaining her uneasiness.

The rooms rented by the Rickets were cheap but pleasantly tidy. Margie invited Cassandra into the drawing room, where some of the items spoke of the Rickets' more affluent past: trinkets from abroad, inlaid coffee table, fine but sadly worn upholstery on the furniture. A screen embroidered with silk peacocks covered the fireplace, and a grand piano stood like an elephant in the room and took up most of the space.

Mrs Ricket, the widow of Nathan Ricket, was having a nap in an armchair near the fireplace. A handkerchief covered her face, rising and falling with her breath. A throng of medicine phials crowded the small table by the side of her armchair.

Margie left Cassandra in the company of the sleeping widow for a moment. She returned with a refined service on a silver tray, another reminder of better days, and stealthily poured tea for Cassandra, so as not to disturb her sleeping mama.

'I don't know who could have done such a thing,' she whispered to the visitor. 'My father wasn't exactly rich or powerful, but he was a decent man. He wouldn't hurt a fly. Who would want to vandalize his grave? I can't even imagine.'

'This is exactly what I'm trying to find out. Do you remember, Miss Ricket, if your father was buried with any valuables?' the detective asked.

'Oh no! When he died, my poor mama and I were left in debt up to our necks,' Margie said with a sad smile. 'My father's business did well. He was an importer. But unfortunately, a fire destroyed his warehouse just before he died. We lost nearly everything overnight. This greatly undermined my father's health.'

The detective took a sip of tea, apologizing with a smile for clinking the cup against the saucer. All the while, Mrs Ricket slept peacefully, snoring quietly, sedated by whatever cocktail of medicine she had been given.

'Does the name Omer Ingleton ring a bell at all, Miss Ricket?'

Margie swallowed her tea and repeated the name, trying to recollect.

'It does sound familiar. Why?'

'Omer Ingleton's grave was also desecrated. Maybe you remember this?' The detective pulled out her notebook and turned to the page with her hand-drawn symbol. 'It was engraved on both Omer Ingleton's and your father's headstones.'

Margie's face lit up.

'Yes! I know what it is.' She raised her voice in excitement, but immediately returned it to a whisper. 'It's a symbol from the seal which was on some of the letters my father used to keep, which reminds me where I saw Mr Ingleton's name: in my father's correspondence.'

'How curious.'

Margie put down her cup and saucer, leapt out of her chair and disappeared into the adjacent room. When she reappeared, she was carrying a stash of letters bound together with a ribbon. She untied it and flipped through the envelopes.

'Here it is. Written to my father by a certain Omer Ingleton,' the young woman said. Mrs Ricket snored a bit louder, disturbed by her daughter's voice. 'But I've never met the man.'

'May I?' Cassandra asked.

Margie handed her the stack. As the detective looked through the letters, she found Nathan Ricket and Omer Ingleton had exchanged quite a number of them, and from a quick look at the contents, it was clear the two men were friends, or even confidantes.

'I've never looked through them. It seemed inappropriate to me. But if it might help...'

'Are these all the letters you're aware of?'

'No, I brought you only one stash. Do you want all of them?'

The young woman again leapt out of her chair and disappeared from the room. This time she returned with a big box full of letters.

CHAPTER 9

The Ghost's Gift

L oaded down with the box of letters and a book she'd newly borrowed from the library, Cassandra approached the superintendent's house. Miss Tesmond was pottering around the flowerbeds in front of the house, murmuring some poetic lines. Her spectacles lay on the open book by her side.

'I didn't know you were a gardener, too,' Cassandra said.

The secretary was startled. She turned around, her cheeks blooming from the cool air.

'Ah! Miss Ayers. Yes, I find it very appealing to get close to nature. It helps me find order in my thoughts.' She tilted her head back to look at the detective from under the wide brim of her hat. 'What is it you're carrying?'

'Just some old letters to read.'

There was something from yesterday's supper that kept nagging at Cassandra. A vague shape lingered at the back of her head like a blur or a phantom before forming into a solid thought. The words casually uttered by Miss Tesmond at the table had been haunting the detective since: 'There must certainly be something to this world beyond that which man's eyes can see.' Cassandra looked at the secretary's spectacles and her suspicion finally shaped. She noticed two men trimming the bushes at the opposite side of the yard.

'And who are they?' She nodded in their direction.

'Oh, just a moment,' Miss Tesmond reached for her spectacles and put them on. 'Oh, that's Willard Simms and Cornelius Mayhew. They're the only two gardeners to stay with us after this bother started. But they only trim the superintendent's garden and don't set foot on the cemetery grounds.'

The secretary replaced her spectacles on the open book and proceeded to cut flowers. Cassandra stood by her side, the magnitude of what she had just seen sinking in.

'Will you find a little time to show me around the cemetery?' she asked. 'I would like to see where you and Ed Brockington encountered the ghost.'

'Yes, of course. I will be glad to help.' Miss Tesmond shook off the dirt from her gardening gloves. 'Just give me a few minutes to tidy myself.'

They agreed to meet at the entrance to the cemetery in an hour. Cassandra went upstairs. In her room, she opened the book she'd brought from the library, a dictionary of symbols. She spent an hour skimming it for the symbol from the Ingleton and Ricket graves, but the search was futile.

* * *

They entered Highgate Cemetery through the arch between two Tudor Gothic chapels – one for Anglicans and the other for Dissenters. In the courtyard, surrounded by the Colonnade, a black horse-drawn hearse with two top-hatted attendants was waiting for its sorrowful burden to be unloaded. Cassandra and Miss Tesmond passed it by in silence and ascended to the burial grounds via the flight of stairs sheltered in the Colonnade.

Tall columns, angels with downcast eyes, Celtic crosses, tombs and gravestones stood in clusters or were scattered among the ferns and ivy along the main path.

'Whenever I am at the cemetery,' the secretary said, 'I always look at the dates when people were born and when they died. I count how many years they lived. Such a sad arithmetic, don't you think?'

Cassandra sighed sagely. From her experience, some lives were too short, but others didn't deserve so many days allotted for their miserable selves, a thought she chose not to voice.

'Forgive me for asking, but it's been bothering me since yesterday,' Miss Tesmond spoke again after a while.

'Ah!' Cassandra knew what was coming.

'Did you really mean what you said about your childhood when you were at the boarding school with Mrs Drummond? Or did you simply want to dazzle the other girls?'

'I was a lonely child, and I spent a lot of time fantasizing,' the detective lied in a confidential tone. 'Lavinia has taken my childish fantasies and converted them into facts. I am sorry I reacted so badly to her mistake.'

Whether Miss Tesmond believed her or not, Cassandra was not going to share any further detail from this chapter of her past.

They walked on in silence until they arrived at the place where the path branched off in two directions: one continued along the lane circumventing the cemetery, the other led to the arch flanked by lotus columns and tall obelisks – the entrance to the Egyptian Avenue.

'That is the Egyptian Avenue.'

'So this is where you saw the ghost?'

'Yes. It was hovering right at the entrance.'

'And where were you?'

The secretary swivelled, recollecting.

'When I woke up from sleepwalking, I found myself here, by Berta Everett's grave.'

Cassandra measured with her eyes the distance from the grave to the arch of the Egyptian Avenue. She wasn't a vision specialist, but the secretary's eyes could hardly see the tip of her own nose, being as she was desperately short-sighted, let alone someone or something standing three hundred feet away in relative darkness.

'Can you remind me what it looked like?' the detective asked.

'It was tall, its silhouette a little transparent and shimmering. I think it was pointing at something, but I was too scared to avert my eyes. I was unable to move.'

'What do you think it was pointing at?'

The secretary's thin shoulders gave a shrug. Cassandra decided that she was either making it all up, or had fallen victim to someone's sick joke. A thorough search around the spot where the ghost allegedly appeared didn't reveal anything. The detective brushed her hand on the tickling branches of the ferns, thinking.

'Let me show you my favourite part of the cemetery.' Miss Tesmond steered her into the Egyptian Avenue. 'Strange as it may sound, though.'

Cassandra followed, limping, her leg stiffening from the long stroll.

'I often come here to draw,' Miss Tesmond said in the dusk of the tunnel.

'What do you draw?'

'Everything. Gravestones, statues, trees.'

They came out of the tunnel, around the Lebanon Circle, and clambered up the stairs to the upper gallery of the cemetery. Miss Tesmond adjusted her pace to Cassandra's, who mounted each step with escalating fatigue. Eventually, they arrived at a Gothic-looking corridor of numerous arches propping up the ceiling. The walls were just like honeycombs divided into small niches for coffins.

'These recesses in which bodies are kept are called *loculi*,' the secretary said, with the peculiar demeanour resembling that of a proud tourist guide.

Cassandra traipsed along the wall, stepping into and out of the shafts of light that penetrated the tunnel through the round openings in the ceiling. The wall looked like a shelf for storing long-forgotten things, except those were not boxes filled with castoffs, but coffins, where people were put, unneeded, like pieces at the end of a chess game – moved, mated, slaid and laid into nicely carved and inlaid boxes. The coffins seemed naked, left there unburied and unprotected, exposed to curious eyes.

* * *

In the dead of the night, Cassandra returned to the cemetery alone to check if someone was making fools of all of them by pulling a trick with a ghost. What else could explain why two completely sane people, Miss Tesmond and Ed Brockington, claimed they had seen it?

A guard post had been abandoned since the supernatural occurrences began – no one was willing to stay at the cemetery after sunset.

In childhood, Cassandra's fear of the dark had been paralysing. When she was six and her mother killed herself, little Cassie became susceptible to the subtle vibrations in the dark; her ears got sharper, picking up on every rustle. Back then, darkness evoked fear so intense it could make her faint. The darkness still scared her, but she had learnt how to put up with it.

For what she saw and heard at night, her elder step-brother called her a lunatic. No one believed her stories, and her father tried to make her stop believing in them, too, by sending her to an asylum in Switzerland, where Dr Bentzel administered his revolutionary treatment – hypnosis. After his sessions, the fear of "sick fantasies" subsided a little; her panic attacks were gone. But even now darkness, or what might be lurking in it, managed to crawl under Cassandra's skin.

The sleuth followed the same path Miss Tesmond had shown her earlier that day; the moonlight helped her find the way. It was remarkable, though, that the secretary could negotiate such a rough and sloppy route while sleepwalking.

The lanes were deserted. At every turn, dark and stooping silhouettes emerged, but as Cassandra drew closer, she discovered them to be statues of angels or mourning maidens. It was even comforting to see them standing like guards along the sides of the alleys. Except for the stone figures, she was alone in the cemetery. Only the hoots of an owl accompanied the crunching sound of her steps.

The Egyptian Avenue was quiet in the worst of ways, that kind of quiet when silence starts whispering in many voices. A sulky place it was – a dark tunnel obscured by the canopy of sprawling vegetation. It resembled a very old medieval street with two rows of doors, except they did not lead to the houses of the living, but to the crypts, the last dwelling of the dead.

After peering into the swelling gloom of the tunnel for what felt like an eternity, Cassandra took a tentative step onto the gravel of the Egyptian Avenue, her every sense alert. The wind slithered low to the ground, rustling the foliage and grabbing her by the ankles as if the fingers of the dead were sprouting from under the soil. Her steps slowed when she managed to bridle her fear, and then quickened when it overwhelmed her again. She wasn't breathing.

Suddenly, one of the crypt doors banged closed. The detective jumped. She bated her breath. The door was rapping furiously against the doorframe as if someone was trying to escape from inside. The detective edged forward so carefully, it was as though she was walking over live coals in her bare feet. She set her hand on the knob. The door continued to protest, albeit mutedly, despite her tight grip. Rat-tat-tat. The sound hypnotized her into a distant memory of the day when an unfortunate accident crippled her for life.

She is thirteen again. Following the fall from the Family Gallery in their mansion, she regains consciousness and opens her eyes to see only a black void. Yet it isn't that thin and dispersed black of a big room where there's still some weak light bouncing from the walls and objects. This particular black, on the contrary, rests like a thick blanket of velvet over the enclosed space. Cassie gropes around. Four walls surround her tightly, hugging her with the comfort of a warm bed. But this is not a room nor bed.

She smells flowers – it is the sickly-sweet odour of lilies. And at this instant it dawns on her where she is. She is inside a coffin! The scent of flowers and the understanding of where she is take away her breath. She goes limp. Then terror seizes her, and she starts to scream, beating the lid of the coffin with her hands and feet, screaming and flailing like an insane creature held captive by the suffocating velvet and silk that has hold of her.

Eventually, exhausted, fingernails bloody, semi-conscious from the lack of air, she sinks into a stupor and awaits her fate. A sound stirs her out of her torpor. She isn't certain but she thinks she hears something. There. It is slight, but there it is again. The sounds of steps, a heavy, shambling gait. An inhuman growl. The girl freezes inside the coffin. Someone outside yanks at the coffin lid, snarling and making disgusting guttural sounds. She clasps both her hands to her mouth, lying quietly with her eyes wide open, staring into the dark nothingness, as someone tugs mightily at the lid, over and over again. She desperately wanted to be found, and now she just as desperately does not. When the lid is finally thrown open with an almighty crash, a face looms over her. A face that causes Cassie to scream herself senseless.

Was it something that really happened, or was it just a dream caused by the turmoil she went through in childhood? Memories never fully returned to her, damaged even more after Dr Bentzel's treatment. Her rational self preferred to think that her traumatized imagination had conjured up all that dread that still haunted her in the night, and there was nothing supernatural to it. She refused to believe in it, and one day she will find all the explanations.

Throwing off this hideous memory with a shake of her head, Cassandra let go of the doorknob, and the door of the crypt resumed its pummelling against the doorframe. It was just the wind.

The Egyptian Avenue eventually ran into the Circle of Lebanon, a circular alley going around a house of crypts in the shape of a drum with an old cedar sitting atop it. The crown of the tree sounded hostile, murmuring in the wind; its branches creaked. Staring at the guardian tree, the detective felt that it was staring back at her.

She was getting cold, and a craving for opium to soothe the shooting pain in her leg. As she turned back, Cassandra heard someone coming from the depths of the Lebanon Circle. She turned slowly at the sound. Someone was within the circle formed by the crypts. The detective squeezed the handle of her stick, peering into the darkness as the steps came nearer and nearer. Someone was going to appear from around the corner any second now, but the steps came to a halt. A tiny and metallic object dropped onto the gravel with a melodic clink. Everything plunged into silence once again.

When Cassandra's heart started beating again, she inched towards the place where she thought she had heard the metal object fall onto the gravel. The shimmering light of the moon helped her locate it. She picked it up, raising it to her eyes. It was a ring, with three rubies set amidst a sprinkle of diamonds. Cassandra felt cold touch her back. It was her mother's ring. The one she had been buried with for over a decade.

'What are you playing at?' she muttered under her breath, but the moonlit cemetery offered no answer.

CHAPTER 10

All My Children Are
Well and Happy

T he next morning another grave was found open at Highgate Cemetery and the coffin in it disturbed. One Emmett Noggs no longer rested in peace. The black pit that had been his retreat for more than half a century was left yawning like a cancerous throat. The symbol of a chalice covered over by a hand was also engraved on his headstone.

It was puzzling to Cassandra how the perpetrator pulled it off right under her very nose while she was patrolling the cemetery. Even more vexing was the fact that whoever did this knew her and took the trouble of retrieving her mother's ring to play this nasty joke on her. Outrageous! To even think that the scoundrel travelled all the way up north, to the Northumbrian coast, and went poking into her mother's grave. Now she would have to send a telegram to Caxton Hall and ask how they could not inform her that her mother's crypt had been vandalized. This meant, of course, she would have to resume her long-lost communication with the family.

Annoyed and frustrated, fumbling with her mother's ring, she was returning from the crime scene when she got a chance to speak to Reverend Gummidge. He had just finished a funeral ceremony at the chapel and was seeing off the relatives of the deceased.

'Good morning, Reverend,' she said, giving way to the cluster of mourners.

'Ah, Miss Ayers.' He shrunk into himself at seeing her and retreated backwards. 'A dreadful business. Have you got any clues yet as to who might have done it?'

'No, not really. In fact, I have a feeling I'm losing my grip,' she sighed, suddenly weary and anxious.

For a long, lingering moment, they stood by the entrance to the Anglican chapel as the light rain drizzled over a moment of weakness the detective was already regretting.

'Are you unwell, Miss Ayers?' the clergyman asked after attentively studying her face.

'No. Yes. But I'll be all right.'

'You know that you can always find comfort in faith.'

'Thank you, Reverend. But comfort is not exactly what I'm looking for.'

'Then, what is it?'

'Truth. Always truth.'

'Ah. Well, truth and comfort don't always go hand in hand.'

'Amen to that. Actually, is there anything more unsettling than the truth? I always dread it the most, the uncovering of it.'

The old man shrugged. 'As one parishioner told me when confessing his sins, *it was worth it*. Is there anything more rewarding than knowing the true reasoning behind people's deeds?' he asked with a smile.

Cassandra raised a surprised look at him.

'You take confessions? How very Catholic of you,' she chuckled.

Reverend Gummidge waved his hand at her in a dismissive manner, though not devoid of friendly irony.

'I know you don't think highly of me, or the Church, for that matter. But I take care of my flock in my way.'

'That I don't doubt.'

With a long stare at each other, they silently agreed to respect each other's antagonism.

'Please.' The reverend invited her to enter the chapel.

The clergyman's sweeping robes rustled behind him as he minced down the aisle. Cassandra ambled in after him. He busied himself with rearranging the flowers near the altar. The detective noted that he had dirt under his nails, rather strange for such a neat man, unless he had dug something out of the ground recently. The reverend followed Cassandra's look and instantly withdrew his hands into his surplice.

'It's not what you are thinking. I was digging some leeks for my dinner. I keep a greenhouse.'

'I wasn't thinking anything, Reverend.' She gave him a comforting smile, but made a mental note, of course. For a change of subject, the detective looked around. 'I forgot how quiet it is in the house of God. I haven't been to a church for many years.'

'Well, that's a shame. You must come and listen to my sermon this Sunday. I will be talking about the importance of serving others.'

'That's an important message if you ask me.' Cassandra paced along the rather simplistic and modestly patterned stained-glass windows. 'But I'm afraid I have a complicated relationship with God.'

'That makes me sad. Then, let me tell you a piece of my sermon now.'

Cassandra wanted to refuse the offer, but the reverend was quick to begin, 'God is not unjust. He will not forget your work and the love you have shown him as you have helped his people and continue to help them. Let this thought raise your spirits.'

'Hebrews 6:10,' the detective assumed.

'You know your Bible, Miss Ayers.' He was pleasantly surprised. 'Very good. Now, I must ask you to excuse me. I have to tend to some arrangements.'

Cassandra recalled something. 'If you have a moment, I'd like to ask you about this symbol.' She retrieved her pocketbook and opened it. 'I have already asked Miss Tesmond, but, sadly, she couldn't find her sketchbook. Do you recognize this image?'

The rough sketch she extended to the reverend showed the

chalice and the protective hand over it. Gummidge's eyes studied the picture.

'This may explain why the graves of the Order members have been opened,' she went on. 'Someone may be looking for hidden treasure in the graves marked by this symbol. But this is only guesswork.'

Realisation dawned on the reverend as he stared at the sketch. He most certainly knew something, and Cassandra was already congratulating herself on a breakthrough, when, despite her expectations, the man shook his head.

'I have no knowledge of this thing. Please, excuse me. I have a lot to do before...'

Without another word, he sidled through the doorway leading to his private quarters. The detective sat down in the pew to rest her aching leg and mull over what she had just seen. Her eyes wandered and finally stumbled upon the man hanging from the cross in front of her. Emaciated and in eternal pain, he stared the other way as if tired by all the shameful deeds he had to witness and all the loss he could not restore.

'I bet you regret how it all turned out. It wasn't worth dying for,' she said to him.

* * *

Autumn indulged Londoners with the last warm days of the year, so the table for luncheon was set in the garden. For Mrs Redlaw, it was an enjoyable ritual she performed with a lot of fuss, during which she poured gossip into her husband's ear while he was trying to read the newspaper.

Wearing a straw hat covered in silk flowers, she was arranging the tea service while her husband was turning the pages, and Cassandra was trying to concentrate on the late Nathan Ricket's letters. The sense of the lines written in his clumsy handwriting was slipping away from her – her mind kept circling back to the previous night in the cemetery. She would gladly believe that it was a sick joke, but the ring was real – it was in her pocket – the ring which had been in her mother's grave for many, many years.

'Such a pity Ellie couldn't join us.' Mrs Redlaw sighed over her cup a moment, after she had expressed how sorry she was for her neighbour Edith Rufford. 'She had to pay a visit to her seriously ill aunt. I asked her if she needed help, but she refused, in an unfailingly polite manner, of course.'

'Doris, darling, you shouldn't be too patronizing with Miss Tesmond. Just leave her be,' was Mr Redlaw's advice. He folded the newspaper, having no chance to read while in his wife's company, and took a tart with berries from the plate she gladly passed over to him.

'I know, but she is such a sweet child. And she loves her aunt dearly. You should have seen the basket she collected for the poor woman: scones, cottage cheese, jam. I think her aunt is having financial difficulties,' she whispered rather loudly.

The expression on Mr Redlaw's face made it clear that he didn't want to hear another word. His wife waved her hand at the thoughts about Miss Tesmond's aunt as if they were annoying flies circling over her head. She clutched the pot and poured more tea for Mr Redlaw and Cassandra. She shot curious glances towards the letters on the detective's lap. With a series of winks, she tried to convince her husband to ask Cassandra about the progress of the investigation. Mr Redlaw pretended not to understand her prompting.

'Whatever is the matter, my darling?' he asked.

Mrs Redlaw rolled her eyes.

'Oh, so much for secrets, Cassie!' she blurted out. 'Tell us what you are reading so eagerly!'

The detective realised just then that she wasn't alone.

'I'm sorry, Mrs Redlaw, but I can't. In due time, I'll tell you everything.'

'I'd be so excited to help the investigation.' The woman shovelled a piece of tart into her mouth, cascades of crumbs falling onto her bosom. She swept them off with a napkin.

Cassandra returned to the letters. One of them managed to seize her attention. It was a letter from Mr Ingleton to Mr Ricket which read, *My dear Nathan, I am back in London. All my children are well and happy to receive all the presents I brought back from India.*

The detective frowned, rereading the passage several times. She felt there was something odd in those lines.

'However, there is a thing you can help me with,' she said.

'Oh?' Mrs Redlaw replaced her cup on the saucer and sat up straight, prepared to listen.

'How many children do you think a man has if he says *all my children are well and happy*?'

The superintendent's wife gave it a very serious consideration, her eyes wandering up in the sky.

'I would say three or more,' was her summary.

'Exactly,' Cassandra agreed. 'A man wouldn't say *all my children* if he had only two of them.'

'It doesn't sound common.'

'It doesn't. Interesting. Considering the fact that Mr Ingleton had only two children; at least, that we know of: Philip Ingleton and Luisa Carstone.'

Puzzled, Mrs Redlaw gave a questioning look to her husband. After waiting for an insufferably suspenseful minute, she asked, 'But what does it mean?'

'It means that, possibly, Mr Ingleton had more children, besides Philip and Luisa. And his friend Mr Ricket was aware of that fact.'

'Mr Ingleton?' the superintendent asked. 'The man whose grave was dug up'

'I'm afraid, yes.'

'Good Lord,' Mrs Redlaw gulped, nearly bursting at the seams with excitement. 'That is scandalous.'

'Though, as they say,' her husband added, *'De mortuis aut bene, aut nihil.'*

'Mr Redlaw is so well-read, isn't he?' she patted her husband on his hand.

'I have another question for you.' Cassandra opened her pocketbook. 'Do you recognize this symbol?'

Both the Redlaws gave the symbol close inspection.

'No, I'm afraid not,' Mrs Redlaw said. 'But you could ask Miss Tesmond. She sketches all those symbols at the cemetery. She must know.'

'Yes, indeed. Well done, darling,' Mr Redlaw said with a broad smile.

But the detective had already asked Miss Tesmond, and Miss Tesmond had already said she knew nothing about the symbol.

An assault of metal jingle-jangle travelled from the inside of the house to the place where the three of them enjoyed their luncheon at the table. Mrs Redlaw winced.

'Oh, that terrible contraption,' she said, meaning the telephone. 'Why would we even install it?'

'It makes things much faster, my dear,' her husband explained.

'Yes. The world wants all things fast today. But at what cost?' She sighed philosophically, voicing one of the retrograde opinions that were common among her generation, and took a big bite off another piece of sponge cake.

The cacophony stopped and they heard the muffled voice of the butler who answered the call. In a moment, he appeared from the French doors that led to the vestibule and carried himself rather gracefully and unhurriedly towards them.

'Who is it, Stubbs?' Mr Redlaw asked.

'It is Mr Duvar calling, sir. He is asking for Miss Ayers.'

'Me?' Cassandra sounded more surprised than she actually was. She knew she would hear from Valentine Duvar sooner or later.

Forced to leave the tea party behind, the detective entered the vestibule of the house, starkly dark after exposure to the daylight. With a reluctant sigh that must have travelled all the way to the other end of the line, she picked up the telephone parts and raised the receiver to her ear and the mouthpiece to her mouth.

'Cassandra Ayers speaking.'

'I've been thinking of you constantly since dinner at the Redlaws. You seemed upset. Was it because I had to leave so early?' The light breath that touched her ear was Valentine's small laugh.

'What is it you want, Mr Duvar?'

'I thought, since I have something you're looking for, you could drop by my photo studio.'

'Listen, I really have no time to...'

'You are still looking for the symbol of the chalice and hand, aren't you?'

She fell silent for a long moment and heard another small laugh on the other end of the line. It seemed Valentine Duvar was very pleased with himself.

'All right, then,' he went on. 'My studio is at 24 Orchard Street. I'll be here all day. You can come anytime.'

CHAPTER 11

Unholy Doings

T he first thing Cassandra noted stepping into Valentine Duvar's studio was that it was rather conventional, with the usual paraphernalia one would expect to see in an ageing bookkeeper's office, but not in the studio of a ghost-chasing photographer. The expensive stationery proudly sat on the reception desk, with a filing cabinet of dark wood next to it. The three rows of dull and unimaginative portrait photographs on the opposite wall were the only feature that betrayed the fact that it was nothing else but a photo studio. The only thing missing was the clerk who would welcome the client, so the detective rang the bell.

Having nothing else to do, Cassandra paced the room, studying its contents and guessing what it all might say about the owner of the place.

The studio was prim and bore no traces of the bohemian lifestyle Valentine had proudly adopted. Perhaps Lord Salisbury, Valentine's father, had a hand in its décor. He wouldn't have let his son disgrace their family by keeping a studio where no decent man would set foot. Of course, that was just a minor battle Lord Salisbury had won in this war between a conservative father and liberal son. The fact that his offspring chose to become a photographer was already disgraceful enough; however, proper appearances were maintained. One of the examples of this was the wall in the parlour, populated with the portraits and crowned with a photograph of the Salisburys, as if it was meant to ward off evil spirits.

Cassandra surmised a potted fern decorating the corner of the room must have been Valentine's mother's doing, as must have been a standing lamp that looked as if borrowed from a lady's boudoir and relegated to the corner to shamefully hang its head in acceptance of its current situation.

After waiting for a while, amused by the observations she had made, Cassandra heard voices and giggling in the back room. She proceeded past a Chinese folding screen of carved dark wood and painted white birds, an exquisite piece a member of the Salisbury dynasty must have brought back from their travels to China.

As she entered, Cassandra was dazzled by a flash. When her sight returned to her, she saw a beautiful woman on a chair, sitting motionless in a pose of bowing and plucking a cello. The setting was adorned in the Empire style and imitated a Georgian hall with portraits and drapings.

'Marvelous!' Valentine said, peeking out at his model from behind the camera.

The woman with the cello woke from her stiff mannequin state and smiled.

'I hope I didn't spoil it,' she said, giggling coquettishly.

'Of course not! How could you?' Passion for his art resonated in Valentine's voice. 'Now, wait a minute. I will adjust the aperture and we will try the other composition.'

'With the candles?'

'Yes, with the candles. Could you, please, put them into the candlestick holders?'

The model's gaze shifted, giving away the presence of somebody behind Valentine's back. He turned around and beamed when he saw Cassandra. He then winced, realising his own forgetfulness, and looked at his watch.

'Is it three already? I'm terribly sorry. I got carried away.'

'So I see,' the detective pursed her lips.

'I will return in a moment,' he promised to the cello player, and came towards Cassandra, raking his reckless curls with his fingers, in an attempt to achieve a more professional look. 'She's my secretary, too,' he nodded in the model's direction.

'Ah.' That was the sound of utter disinterest. 'Mr Duvar, you said you knew what the symbol was. I wouldn't like to rob you of your time.'

'Of course, you wouldn't.' A smirk touched one corner of Valentine's mouth. He directed Cassandra towards his office with an outstretched arm. 'Shall we?'

This was where Valentine's true character was imprisoned. This was his treasure trove. His office resembled a loud and vivid back room of a cabaret, with eclectic furniture, costumes hanging from the racks, all sorts of props and the more unconventional photographs than those Cassandra had seen at the entrance. In these photographs you could see the display of scandalous characters, suggestive attires and frivolous poses. But that was not all. Some of the images were of shiny spheres and transparent ghostly figures.

'So what do you think of this?' Valentine asked.

'I know all the optical tricks that create illusions like this. You won't make me believe they are real.'

'No. I don't mean the pictures. I mean me,' he spread his arms showing himself in all his glory.

'What are you...?'

'I mean, what is your judgment of me?'

'What makes you think I have one?'

'You are clearly passing a judgment about me right now in your pretty little head. So what's the verdict?'

'I don't judge people,' she replied, pretending to be interested in the photographs.

'At least I know a little more about you now,' he said, rummaging through a pile of clothes and hats on his desk.

'What's that?'

'I know that you are a poor liar.'

'I beg your pardon?'

'I think the truth is, you judge people all the time.' Valentine retrieved a big yellow envelope from under the heap of costumes. A men's boot fell on the floor with a muffled thud. He extended the envelope to Cassandra. 'Also, I think, most of the time, you don't really like what you see in them.'

The detective made a face that was intended to show how skeptical she was about his attempt to peg her genuine nature. She pulled at the envelope in his hand, but he did not let go.

'Am I right?'

'Well, you got me.' She tugged at the envelope harder and snatched it out of his grip.

It was not sealed, so Cassandra easily fished out a portrait photo of an elderly and stern-looking man.

'What am I looking at?' she asked.

'Here.' Valentine pointed at the badge on the man's lapel.

Cassandra raised the picture closer to her eyes and squinted: the symbol on the badge was a chalice with a hand over it.

'It can't be. Where did you get this?'

'One of my clients,' he explained. 'I took this photo right in this studio a few days ago. His name is Arthur Chillingwood. He is also known as Baron Hexam.'

'What does the symbol on his lapel mean?'

'I wasn't sure, so I asked my father. He says this is the coat of arms of an old secret society, the Order of Holy Protectors.'

'I've never heard of them.'

'Well, that is the main point of a secret society, isn't it?'

'Go on,' Cassandra told him, bringing the photograph of Baron Hexam closer to her eyes.

'I don't know much, only that the Order came into existence in the times of the Reformation, when Thomas Cromwell destroyed the Catholic monasteries.'

'So, since they are a religious order, Reverend Gummidge *must have* known something about them when I asked him.'

'Well...' There was hesitation in Valentine's voice.

'Well, what?'

'According to my father, and I quote, "They are a knot of

idlers who sit in their fancy salons, smoking cigars, pretending to be the protectors of the Holy Church and babbling on about treasure like some silly old spinsters.'"

'Treasure?' The detective woke up from thinking about the conversation with the reverend the day before.

'They must have some. The Order safely hid away the riches of some of the major monasteries before they could be taken by Cromwell.'

'But of course. This might explain why the graves of the former Order members have been opened. Someone may be looking for the hidden treasure.'

'Oh. I see. Jolly good. Tell me more!'

'Have you got his address?' The detective pointed at the man in the picture.

'Yes, I have. But the old chap leads a very secretive life and doesn't see anyone. He will receive me, though, because I am his photographer and,' Valentine left the best part for the end, 'he's my godfather.'

The moment lingered while Cassandra took in the meaning of his words.

'What do you want, Mr Duvar?'

'Make me your partner,' he said matter-of-factly.

The woman chortled and headed for the door, brushing past him like a gust of Nordic wind.

'Thank you for your help. I'll do the rest myself.'

'Old Chillingwood is a tough man. He won't even let you near the gate of his house.'

This made the sleuth hesitate at the door and turn back around, still weighing the need to resort to assistance from the annoying photographer. Valentine picked up the boot that had fallen out of the pile of costumes and shoved it back into the bundle. He looked at his visitor with a victorious smile.

'All right,' Cassandra said reluctantly. 'I will let you shadow me while I'm on this case. But when I'm done with it, we part ways.'

'Deal,' he reached out to shake her hand. 'You will be the

first private detective with your own photographer. You'll see it might come in handy. You won't regret it, Miss Ayers.'

'That's exactly what I'm doing right now. Please, Mr Duvar, don't turn my investigation into a spectacle,' she said, and turned once again towards the door.

On their way back to the parlour, they discussed a good time to pay a visit to Baron Hexam the next day, when they stopped in front of the portraits lining one of the walls. The sight of the elegantly dressed people, in their rigid poses and with void expressions on their faces, gave Cassandra an idea.

'By the way, Mr Duvar, since I'm here, I might as well use your services,' she said.

'My services?'

'I'd like to send my family a photo of me. It's a small price to pay in exchange for not having to go there myself.'

'You want me to take a picture of you?' He might sound less surprised if she proposed to him.

'Yes. It is what you do here, isn't it?'

'Of course. I'd be delighted.' He invited her back into the studio with a gesture of his hand. 'Would you like to try on a costume? You can choose anything, from Cleopatra to a Danish mermaid.'

'Let's not go crazy. Just a usual photograph, as... *normal* as the ones from the parlour.'

'Normal it shall be.'

* * *

Later that day, after a sumptuous dinner in the company of the Redlaws and Miss Tesmond, Cassandra retreated to her room where her smoking set waited for her. The whole day of walking resulted in a terrible pain in her bad leg. Pale and exhausted, she endured the dinner out of sheer politeness. But before she allowed herself to use the opium, and whilst her mind was still sharp, she sat at the desk and prepared sheets of paper to help her organize her thoughts. Visual cues enhanced her thinking process.

On the first sheet, she drew a caricature of Philip Ingleton and Luisa Carstone – Philip as a cricket of a man with a high, starched collar, and Luisa as a crowned toad in an armchair. On the second sheet, glasses and a high bun of hair portrayed Miss Tesmond. Hands latching onto a Bible represented Reverend Gummidge on the third piece of paper.

She had just started a sketch of Margie Ricket, chubby cheeks under a funny ruffle of a cap, when a draft touched her shoulders. What really gave her chills, though, was the sound that wafted in from the side of the cemetery – a man was bawling at the top of his lungs.

Someone ran past Cassandra's room in the direction of the stairs. She lifted the lower panel of the sash window just in time to see Mr Redlaw in his dressing-gown, dashing across the yard, with a lantern in one hand and a gun in the other. He was heading for the cemetery, his valet, Palmer, at his heels.

Cassandra threw on her coat and ran out of her room. A commotion stirred behind every door as all the inhabitants of the house who had been preparing for sleep were now hurriedly pulling on their robes and opening their doors.

The detective rushed all the way to the cemetery. Her lungs throbbed from the icy night air. The darkness pulsated menacingly. She stopped only when she reached the place where the path branched off in two different directions. She waited for some noise or movement to provide a hint as to where to go next. Nothing except her own breathing. She swivelled in frustration, wandering around, gnawing at her lips. In her gut, she had a feeling that something irreversible had happened, and that somehow she was to blame for it.

The arch of the Egyptian Avenue loomed in the dark, its tunnel, like jaws of a monster, open to devour anyone who dared come closer. Seeing a gleam from a lantern on the opposite side of the Egyptian Avenue, Cassandra ventured into the darkness of the tunnel.

It was pitch-dark inside. Anything or anyone could be lurking in the shadows, and she wouldn't even know. She could see only the exit where the darkness was less dense, drenched with moonlight.

Her ears caught the sound of gravel crunching to her left. The woman froze, peering into the haunted void. Her nose picked up the scent of tobacco and dirt. Cassandra raised her cane and with it prodded the dense and wobbling darkness. Nothing.

Mr Redlaw was coming back. He entered the tunnel, the lamp swaying before his face, etched with shock from whatever it was he had just witnessed.

'Miss Ayers, do *not* go down there,' the superintendent said, his voice hoarse. 'I'm sending for the police.'

As he brushed past her, his lamp filled the tunnel with yellow light. She could see clearly there was no one inside except the two of them. One of the crypt doors lining the walls on both sides was pounding against the doorframe. Mr Redlaw hesitated for a moment.

'I insist you accompany me back to the house, Miss Ayres,' the superintendent said, walking away. 'It's not safe here.'

'Why? What happened?'

'A dreadful thing.'

The man did not say, but he did not have to. Cold and sticky suspicion of the worst kind had already crept up on Cassandra.

'No,' she said. 'I need to be here and gather all the evidence if you want me to solve the case.'

'I'm afraid it's up to the police now. Vandalism is one thing, but this... What was I thinking? I should have reported it to Scotland Yard weeks ago.'

Cassandra felt a pang from a disappointment she may have caused him. Of course, she was not in possession of the resources Scotland Yard had, but her wits were second to none, including any man in a police uniform.

'I still want to see everything with my own eyes,' she insisted.

Mr Redlaw let her proceed with a nod of his head.

When the detective came out from the tunnel and circumvented the Lebanon Circle, she saw the light of Palmer's lantern hanging among the headstones on the upper gallery, and walked towards him.

'Who's there?' the man asked from above.

'It's me, Palmer.' The woman ascended the stairs to the upper gallery. Mr Redlaw's valet was standing in the pool of light shed by his lantern, nervously keeping watch. He dabbed at the sweat on his forehead with a handkerchief.

The first thing Cassandra noticed was a heap of dirt from another unearthed grave and a man's feet sticking out from behind a nearby granite sarcophagus. She hoped the body had been exhumed, but it was not in the least decomposed, and belonged to a man who had been alive just moments before.

As if reading Cassandra's thoughts, Palmer shook his head in answer to her silent question as to whether the victim on the ground was still alive. She drew closer to the body. It was Reverend Gummidge lying there. Dead. Exposed to the moonlight, his face resembled a mask of horror. His right hand still clasped a spade.

'There may be footprints.' The detective searched for them under her feet, but the patch of ground had already been stomped over by Mr Redlaw and Palmer.

'Look at his face. He died from fright,' the valet said, shaking.

Cassandra picked up her petticoats and climbed up to the rim of the granite sarcophagus so as not to further obliterate any traces left by the murderer.

'May I?' she reached out for the lantern.

Palmer passed it to her. She raised the lantern to the headstone of the grave that had been dug out. There was the chalice and the hand of the Order of Holy Protectors engraved upon it.

'Would never think it was the reverend who had been desecrating the graves. The ghost killed him for his unholy doings,' the valet said quietly, as if uneasy about Reverend Gummidge still eavesdropping and passing his judgment on him.

'I am not so sure about that.' The detective examined the

reverend's head. She turned it carefully and revealed a deep wound and blood smeared all over his cheek and temple. She also took note of the spade. It was covered in dirt but there was no blood on it. The perpetrator had taken the murder weapon with them.

By the time an inspector and two constables from Scotland Yard arrived, Cassandra had seen enough. She strolled back to the superintendent's house, armed with Palmer's lantern. Its light sprawled across the walls of the Egyptian Avenue. She checked to see if she could detect any footprints, but the gravel-coated path revealed nothing.

When searching along the wall, she tried the door of the crypt that kept banging and it appeared to be unlocked. As though she was opening the gates to hell, the door let out a loud creak as Cassandra pushed it open. Inside the crypt was a perfect place to hide.

After a brief inspection of the crypt, the detective spied something on the floor. She bent over a tiny pinch of burnt tobacco. She carefully brought her finger to it – the tobacco was still warm. Someone had been here only a moment before she arrived.

CHAPTER 12

The Great Magister

'Poor fool!' Cassandra thought while watching from her window as the constables bundled the reverend's body into the patrol wagon. 'Poor greedy fool!'

She sat at the tea table in the company of subdued Mrs Redlaw and Miss Tesmond, and watched through the French door as the chief inspector from Scotland Yard questioned the superintendent of the cemetery. One of the constables from the night before stood at his side and scribbled down the answers.

Cassandra was also taking her notes, writing down the most valuable observations: "killed with a blow to his head," "the same symbol on the headstone," "the spade is covered in dirt, but no traces of blood." She hesitated before writing down the last one: "He knew about the symbol when I asked him."

Obviously, the clergyman had guessed it was all about the Order of the Holy Protectors, and that the culprit might have been looking for the Order's treasure in the graves of its former members, so he had decided to try his luck. Who wouldn't want to lay their hands on the priceless artifacts? Alas, as it turned out, he hadn't been the only one at the cemetery that night, and certainly not the greediest one. Did it make her culpable in Gummidge's death? She could have insisted on him telling her what he knew about the Order, but she didn't press him on the matter.

It was up to her to look for the symbol in the libraries,

to check the guides and directories. There must have been something about the Order in the books and chronicles, but if not, she would have to go and see her old friend who was an archivist working in Parliament. She had a feeling Reverend Gummidge was up to something when she last talked to him. She should have prevented him from doing anything foolish.

The reverend's death was a difficult blow to the dwellers of the superintendent's house. All morning, Mrs Redlaw sniffed at smelling salts and vigorously waved her fan, promising everyone she was going to faint any moment, though she remained conscious enough to barrage every living soul in her immediate vicinity with endless questions. Every detail over which she could moan and sob was worthy of hearing.

'It's so, so awful,' Mrs Redlaw sniffed into her handkerchief. Her face was streaked red with tears. 'Yesterday the poor thing dined with us and complimented my cook on the quails, and today he is lying cold in that horrible wagon, all alone. He loved company so much.'

Cassandra winced as the incessant moaning seemed to reverberate in unison with the voice of her own remorse.

'I won't be able to say a word for days,' the mistress of the house went on.

'Wouldn't that be great,' the detective thought, covering her already written notes with new layers of ink, unable to focus on anything because of Mrs Redlaw's blabbering.

'What an atrocious business. Lucy! Come here, girl! We need to start planning the wake for our poor old chap. Lucy! Where is that girl?'

Miss Tesmond flinched at the woman's high-pitched voice, as the latter rose to her feet and walked out of the room, looking for the maid.

'I'm sorry you had to see the murder scene,' the secretary said to Cassandra. 'That must have been horrible.'

'You have nothing to be sorry about. It wasn't you who killed him, was it?'

'Me? Oh! Um. No, of course not.'

The detective studied her with an intent stare. Why was she constantly haunted by the feeling that everyone was lying to her? Whether Scotland Yard was looking into it or not, Cassandra was going to uncover the truth, even if the case of the Highgate ghost was no longer about vandalism. Someone capable of murder was at large, and she had to catch them before it became a killing spree. The prospect of finding thousands of pounds of treasure is a very strong motivator for engaging in nefarious activities. Anyone could venture into a dangerous game.

The first step was to talk to a member of the Order – better still, to the head of it – and hear what they had to say about the treasure allegedly hidden in their former members' graves. She was lucky that Valentine had informed her about his godfather. Unfortunately, the explanations she might get from Baron Hexam would not change the fate bestowed upon Reverend Gummidge. That was poor timing, and time is an effortless murderer.

Her attention was drawn to some of Nathan Ricket's and Omer Ingleton's letters tucked in between the pages of the notebook. The address on every one of the envelopes was the same – 62 Pont Street in Knightsbridge. It did not match either the address of Ingleton's townhouse or the one where Margie Ricket now lived. It could mean the address where both men had been sending their letters was their common meeting place, a headquarters perhaps. Cassandra had heard that secret organizations often used a dummy address for receiving their mail, where some unsuspecting dupe lived and received the correspondence on their behalf.

When later that day Valentine Duvar took her to the place where Baron Hexam lived, she noted with frustration that the address was exactly 62 Pont Street in Knightsbridge, a terraced house opposite St Columba's Church. What an idiot she was that it had not occurred to her to check the address.

'Is everything all right?' Valentine asked, while she was paralysed with the realisation of her own horrible mistake and stood staring at a neat house of greenish-brown brick, with a stately white porch.

'Shall we?' She proceeded towards the entrance flanked by two bushes in pots, trimmed into spiky forms.

The second-floor terrace was decorated with lush potted plants. Through the windows, one could see the showy display of rich curtains and exquisite décor. However, nothing in the aspects of the house gave any indication that it was different from any other house in Knightsbridge.

Cassandra climbed up the five steps to the entrance door, leaning heavily on her walking stick, and raised her hand to the knocker in the shape of a lion baring its teeth.

'Before we go in there,' Valentine said, clinging to the envelope with the photograph, 'I must warn you that my godfather is not the nicest person.'

'Don't worry. Dealing with people who are not so nice is my profession.'

'No. You don't understand. How can I put it? Say King Herod is nothing compared to him.'

'I'm sure you're painting the devil blacker than he is.'

'The devil is another good reference in describing Hexam.'

Cassandra made a skeptical face at him and knocked on the door with the lion's head.

'Don't forget about our agreement,' she added. 'You introduce me, but I interview His Lordship myself.'

'Be my guest.' From his tone it was clear he anticipated the worst.

'Yes?' A man, too young to be a butler, so perhaps a footman, stuck his nose through the crack in the door. He first saw Cassandra but then recognized Valentine. 'Ah, Mr Duvar.'

'Good day, Terrence.'

However, the footman did not let them in, guarding the door as firmly as a hellhound. 'And this is?' he asked, looking down at the stranger.

'Cassandra Ayers, my good friend,' Valentine introduced her.

'You know, Mr Duvar, His Lordship does not see any visitors.'

'Yes. I know. But I'm here to deliver His Lordship's photograph.' He showed the envelope to the footman.

'I will pass it to him,' Terrence extended his hand.

After an awkward beat, having depleted reasons for them to enter the house, Valentine surrendered the delivery to the footman. The door started to close, but Cassandra shot out her foot to block the door from closing. The scowl on the footman's face was only half visible through the opening.

'I'm a private detective. I'm investigating the desecration of the graves at Highgate Cemetery. Could I speak to the owner of the house?'

The response was already on the footman's lips. 'I am sorry, madam, but it's out of the question.'

'Two men whose graves were defiled were Nathan Ricket and Omer Ingleton. Their mutual correspondence used to be sent to this address.' She brandished the envelope under his nose. 'I need to speak to Baron Hexam, or he will have to speak with the police.'

The footman's heavy gaze lingered on the detective.

'One moment, please.' He looked down at her foot in the door. She looked down, too, and then back up at the young man. Reluctantly, she withdrew her foot to allow the door to close.

Valentine flashed an impressed smile at Cassandra.

'So that's how you do this? Just put your foot in the door and threaten the homeowners?'

'If that's what it takes to get the information I need.'

'How bold of you.'

Clumsy drops of rain created an impressionist picture on the pavement at their feet while they were waiting.

'It wasn't always like that. When I just started and was on my first case, people would shut their doors in my face all the time. Everyone hates being asked questions about their lives and skeletons being taken out of their closets. So I soon realised, you just do whatever it takes to pass through the door: you ask politely, persuade, plead, threaten or ram the damn door down if it's needed. Because if you don't do this, you won't stop the perpetrator: something will be stolen again, another life will be ruined, another woman will be raped or worse – someone will get killed. And you will be blaming yourself for the rest of your life for not trying hard enough to get through the bloody door.'

'I say,' was Valentine's quiet response. 'I hope you don't blame yourself for the reverend's demise. Blame me if you want. I came forward too late with the information about the symbol.'

A sad smile touched Cassandra's lips.

'Blaming oneself is a very addictive practice, Mr Duvar. Once tasted, it takes over and clouds your better judgment.'

The footman was back, peeking through the door.

'I'm afraid we cannot help you,' he said, and started to close the door when the detective threw her foot in it.

When people refused to talk to her, it usually meant that she was getting closer. She was not going to let this opportunity go.

* * *

Arthur Chillingwood, or Baron Hexam, received them while sitting at the desk in his office. He hardly even looked at them as he was scribbling something in a bookkeeping ledger. Footman Terence left, closing the doors behind him as if leaving the visitors in a cage with a wild and ferocious animal.

Cassandra and Valentine exchanged a look and took a seat in the armchairs across from the baron, although they were not invited to do so. The man stooped over his desk and screeched away with his pen. The sound made Cassandra flinch. She felt like it wasn't paper but her very marrow he was writing on.

As the bookkeeping was still in progress, the detective used the time to look around. Arthur Chillingwood's study at 62 Pont Street was obviously the heart of the Order's headquarters. All the bookcases were padlocked, and the books within had no names on their spines. The mantelpiece seemed suspiciously empty; clean circles in the very thin layer of dust indicated that some objects had been hurriedly put away before the unwanted guests' attendance. Around the baron's neck, a pendant with the chalice and protective hand caught the sunlight.

Chillingwood raised his eyes and muttered while he finished

writing some lines. 'This is not your bohemian lair, boy. You can't bring your folk here whenever it pleases you.'

'Forgive me. I didn't want to be presumptuous...' Valentine started.

The old man laughed croakily.

'Yet you were.'

'Miss Ayers has very important business she'd like to discuss with you, so I thought...'

'Keep in mind for the future that it is I who decides what business can be discussed under this roof.' The old man delivered the words with curtness and spoke with a distinctly Scottish burr.

'Sure.'

'It is not quite true, Your Lordship,' Cassandra interfered, and the cold stare of Baron Hexam shifted from Valentine to her. 'A man has been killed. It got the attention of Scotland Yard and thus the attention of the Crown. You don't say you are reluctant to help the investigation if it's in the interest of the king, do you?'

'I don't see any Scotland Yard's beagles at my door. Only you.'

'I'm ahead of the investigation.'

'Why wouldn't you share the precious knowledge you have with the police, then, if you care so much about the interests of the Crown?' He pointed his index finger at her as if he had uncovered her secret. 'Ah. Ambition. That's what it's all about. Not some clergyman's life. You're simply trying to prove yourself. To your family. To the entire retched world. But most of all to yourself. You fight your little battles. Isn't that right?'

Cassandra ignored his one-eye-squinted glare, sick of the people who pretended they could read her like an open book, who dared say they knew something about her "battles." The baron put the pen aside and locked his fingers together in front of him on the desk. 'I understand that Lord Dunstan is your father,' he went on. 'May I ask how he takes your mode of life? This lady detective nonsense?' He made a dismissive little gesture with his hand.

'I haven't come here to discuss my relationship with my

father, sir.'

'Oh. He must be so very disappointed.' A toad-like smirk curved the baron's lips.

Valentine visibly shrunk in his armchair. Cassandra, on the contrary, took out a cigarette and lit it, not an inch destabilized by what Hexam had just said. If he wanted to throw her off guard or embarrass her, he should have tried harder. She was immune to patriarchal rage and opinions no one asked for.

'My father is disappointed, all right. But the feeling is mutual. Now, before we start enjoying this conversation too much, I need to ask you some questions, Your Lordship.'

'It is my right to not answer any of them.'

'Four graves have been defiled at Highgate Cemetery,' she said, her breath coming out of her lungs with a plume of smoke.

'What a rotten business. Where do I come into this matter?'

'It appears that the desecration of the graves is tied to the Order, the members of which were buried in all four graves in question. By the members I mean Omer Ingleton, Nathan Ricket, Emmett Noggs and Reed Dartle, all of whom, I'm sure, you know well. From Margie Ricket, Nathan Ricket's daughter, I received letters which prove that Ingleton and Ricket were friends, but, strangely, all their letters were sent to this address.'

Cassandra held up the bunch of envelopes.

'So what?' Chillingwood defensively jutted out his lower jaw. 'They may have lived here.'

'I've checked it, sir. They didn't. You've owned this house for decades. However, they certainly came here now and then to collect their correspondence. I suspect this is the headquarters of the Order, and you are its magister.'

'Believe it all you want!' he burred.

'The investigation could use your help. A man has been killed.'

Chillingwood shrugged his shoulders indifferently. 'We are all mortal.'

'The perpetrator is looking for something in the Order's graves, treasure perhaps. It may cast a shadow on the members of the Order, as only the insiders can be aware of the treasure.' She stubbed the cigarette into the ashtray on Chillingwood's desk. 'Think what damage it will do to your little secret society if the gossip spreads.'

The baron's squinted eye narrowed even more, emitting almost tangible cold.

'Are you threatening me?'

'Threatening? No. I'm simply giving you a perspective. And it might be rather bleak if I resort to the help of the press. They love stories like this. Murder, secret order, treasure. It'll make the front page.'

'What is your proof?' he spat.

'Please, it is the press, not a court. They'll grab any sensational news and ask for more.' Cassandra stood up, pulling on her leather gloves, and headed for the door. Valentine, unsure about his role in the unfolding situation, followed her awkwardly.

'All right. All right,' Chillingwood said through his teeth. 'She wants to know about the treasure.'

He sprang to his feet. The visitors drew back as Baron Hexam brushed past them and approached the bookcase. He yanked at its doors, but they didn't yield. Huffing and puffing, the old man rang the bell to summon the servant.

'Give me the key!' he demanded, veins in his neck swelling, when Terrence appeared in the doorframe.

'The key, My Lord?' The young man grasped at a ring with a bunch of keys attached to his belt.

'To this!' Chillingwood waved at the bookcase, forgetting the word. 'What do you call it?'

'The bookcase? You need the key to the bookcase?'

'No, to the pearly gates of heaven!'

'But you never gave it to me, My Lord.' The footman took a tiny step towards his master and whispered, 'You always keep it on the chain.'

The baron fished out the key on a chain from under his shirt, slightly embarrassed by his own forgetfulness. He shoved the key in Terrence's hand.

All the time the footman was poking in the keyhole with the key and getting it jammed, Chillingwood's chest was puffing out under the tweed of his jacket as if he were a bird growing in size to strike fear into its enemy. After jiggling the key in the keyhole, the bookcase was successfully opened.

'Get that lock fixed, Terrence,' the baron spat. 'You put me in an embarrassing situation.'

'Yes, My Lord.'

'You may go.'

The footman stepped out of the room.

Chillingwood grabbed a massive volume from the shelf. Its cover read

"The Holy Protectors Chronicle." He licked his index finger and paged through the book, mumbling some curses.

'Here!' He shoved the book into the detective's hands. 'The list of all items saved from the monasteries and hidden by the Order. And here...' Before the woman managed to read even a single line, he started shuffling the pages again and stopped at a different document. 'This states that the Order committed all its fortune to the Crown. Signed by the fifteenth Magister of the Order in 1712.'

The book included a copy of the document, signed and sealed.

'So the Order doesn't have any treasure?' the detective asked.

'No treasure; at least, not any that I am or anyone else in the Order is aware of.'

Cassandra stopped for a moment, pondering.

'Then, it seems, Your Lordship, there are two possibilities here.' She held up two fingers. 'One, our perpetrator isn't aware of this act.' She nodded at the book. 'Or two,' she said, holding up her second finger, 'there's some treasure still hidden which was not committed to the Crown.'

Still breathing heavily, Chillingwood looked intently at Cassandra. He tried to hide the fact that the detective's conclusion got him listening, but he was hit hard with her deduction, and it was written all over his face.

'You got what you wanted. Now, get out,' he hissed.

There was no need to ask twice. Footman Terrence saw the visitors out and shut the door behind them. The locks and latches snapped loudly inside, sealing the house from the prying world.

'Well, that was a success,' Cassandra concluded as she walked down the porch.

'Speak for yourself. I didn't get paid for the photograph.' Valentine shoved his hands into the pockets of his trousers and followed his limping partner at a loose-limbed gait.

'You'd take money from your godfather?'

'Have you seen the chap? To charge him twice the price is the only pleasure I get from it. He's a wild boar. By the way, I'm sorry he spoke about your family.'

'No need to apologize. In fact, I enjoyed the conversation.'

'You're joking, right? What was there to enjoy?'

'You clearly don't know a thing about people, Mr Duvar. Do not be afraid of the man who shows his anger; beware of the one who hides it. Your godfather is just an old grump. A harmless grump. Stay-away-not-to-spoil-the-day type. But we are after someone who hides in plain view, with whom you talk about the weather and shake hands, maybe even dine with at one table, having no idea this person is capable of murder. That is a scary thought, isn't it?'

'Certainly unnerving. I'll refrain from shaking hands these days.'

They proceeded down the street, passing by the flower vendor and two nannies cooing over a baby in a pram. Checking the road for any traffic before crossing, Cassandra noticed a secret smile playing on Valentine's lips.

'What is that happy face all about?'

'Oh. Nothing, really.'

They crossed the cobbled street, carefully avoiding the horse dung spread all over it.

'It's just...' Valentine went on. 'You said, "*we* are after

someone." I take it as a sign that you accepted our partnership.'
   'Take it as you wish,' the detective rolled her eyes.

CHAPTER 13

All Suspects

The ointment of camphor, mustard powder, spirit and egg yolks soothed Cassandra's knee and ankle with a pleasant chill. She massaged it, rubbing the ointment in, and then wrapped her leg in a towel.

She had a better remedy, though. Installed comfortably by the fireplace in her room at the superintendent's house, she took a pull on the smoking pipe; the opium surged through her body, relieving her pain. It softened the painfully spiky sphere of her memories into a ball of yarn she was struggling to untangle.

After a brief nap, the detective returned to the case. She laid out the caricatures of the suspects and the pictures of the important details she had drawn previously: four images for the four vandalised graves with the names of the deceased on the headstones; an image each for the murdered Reverend Gummidge, Miss Tesmond, Margie Ricket, Mr and Mrs Redlaw, the Ingletons, Ed Brockington, Harmon and the other groundsmen she had spoken to.

Margie or her family could have knowledge of the treasure and be hunting for it. They could certainly do with some financial aid, considering their constrained means. The Ingletons were definitely holding something back. Those two would not shun even the grimmest business for the sake of a penny. But they would have probably hired someone to do the job. Some groundsmen, maybe? Cassandra sighed at her own bias; she admitted there was no other indication of the Ingletons' implication except her own dislike of them.

'Come on, girl. You're better than this,' she mumbled and put the Ingletons' caricatures aside.

 Although kindhearted and welcoming, the Redlaws had every opportunity to determine where the Order's burial plots were. They also had easy access to the cemetery by day and at night. Of course, it was the superintendent himself who hired her to work the case. Why would he do that if he was involved? However, Cassandra had a case before where the perpetrator turned out to be the very person who told her about the crime in the first place. It was 1897, the case of a kidnapped scullery maid. According to the master of the house, the gypsies who stayed at the edge of his property befuddled the poor girl with their magic and she ran away with their tribe. Alas, there was no magic and no romance – only the master's sharp razor on the maid's throat and a deep abandoned well.

Cassandra reminded herself that she could not rely on her likes and dislikes as well as on the impressions people were trying to create. The last time she fell into this trap was a year ago when she investigated a simple case of a stolen brooch, and it nearly spiralled into a grisly murder. No more feelings, only deduction, only evidence; at least they don't lie and don't pretend to be something else.

What about Miss Tesmond? She certainly spent a lot of time strolling around the cemetery and making sketches. She could have seen something or discovered something by accident.

Or maybe Arthur Chillingwood, a.k.a. Baron Hexam, had something to do with the desecration of the graves. He knew the members of the Order and where they were buried. Cassandra made a sketch of Chillingwood – a one-eye-squinted man with stag's antlers as a symbol of a proud dynasty. No, he couldn't. The whole idea of the treasure hunt came unexpected to him, that was obvious. But was it, really? Or was he putting on an act?

'Ugh.' She stretched her stiff leg.

For a long while, she reclined in the armchair and stared at the drawings now covering the table like a tablecloth. She had to look for those who withheld from her, those who were guarding their secrets. Alive or dead.

Philip Ingleton and his sister Luisa were reluctant to speak about their father, and pretended they didn't know anything about the coat of arms engraved on their father's headstone. Why were they so unconcerned about the horrible desecration of their father's grave? Cassandra was almost certain Omer Ingleton had two sets of children. Where could the other Ingleton children be now? Did they know about the Order? The detective isolated the card of Philip and Luisa Ingleton.

And then there was the ghost. Two people had seen it, or, at the least, were made to believe they'd seen it: Miss Tesmond and Ed Brockington. Cassandra put their cards aside. Something wasn't right about Ed Brockington. She closed her eyes, trying to recollect the details of the day she had met Ed Brockington. Dilapidated garden – strange for a gardener. Perhaps it was a case of the shoemaker's children having no shoes. Perhaps. Then there was that neat basket with food amidst the mess of his house – he must have a caring woman somewhere. His skin was unusually, exotically sun-tanned, while his face reminded her of a pirate. She added an eye patch to the caricature of Ed Brockington.

There was something at the back of her memory that had not surfaced yet. It was time to take measures, before the business took another nasty turn.

* * *

'Tell me again, why are we doing this?' Valentine put his bulky camera on the tripod in front of the Ingletons' house while Cassandra watched the road.

'There is one thing these people are afraid of most of all.'

'Cameras?'

'Exposure, Mr Duvar. Now, do your job, please.'

'And this helps us how?' He went on setting up the apparatus.

An elegant carriage drawn by four first-rate horses pulled up at the porch.

'They are here,' the detective said. 'You ready?'

Valentine armed himself with a flashlamp.

A footman unfolded the steps of the carriage and opened the door. Philip Ingleton's grasshopper face emerged from the dark interior; his big teeth were naked in a smile of a person who was as yet oblivious as to how his day was about to be ruined. As soon as he saw Cassandra looming on the porch, his face became sour.

Philip was helping his sister out of the plush of the carriage and throwing befuddled looks at the detective and her photographer. Their butler slipped out of the house, past Cassandra and Valentine, and hurried to explain everything to his master.

'I told her that you wouldn't receive her, sir, but she wouldn't listen.'

'All right, all right, Ogbourne. Don't sweat so much. It's not your fault.'

'Not his fault?' Luisa wheeled at him. 'Why didn't you call the police, you old fool?'

'What does this woman want?'

At Cassandra's nod, Valentine opened the lens of the camera and fired the flashlamp at them, capturing their outrage in a photograph. The attention of the neighbourhood, represented by the two respectable gentlemen on the other side of the street and a scullery maid scurrying past on errands, was drawn to the unusual scene.

'What in the name of..?' Philip advanced towards the assailants of his property, still slightly blinded by the flashlight.

'This is Mr Murphy.' The detective waved her hand at Valentine. 'He is with the Daily Telegraph.'

'What is that supposed to mean?'

'The Daily Telegraph is interested in your story. They would like to boost it to the national scale.'

'What is this woman talking about?' Luisa grabbed her brother by his arm. Her eyes went wildly wide. Philip, in contrast, squinted suspiciously.

'Listen, I don't know whom you were talking to...'

'Let the dead speak for themselves,' Cassandra said. She unfolded Omer Ingleton's letter and read, 'My dear Nathan, I am back in London. My role in the creation of the Indian National Congress is complete and I don't think I will be coming back, although this wonderful country will forever stay in my heart. But it is good to be home again. All my children are well and happy to receive the presents I brought back from my travels. All of them are simply the most adorable things in the world.'

The detective took a pause to check the expressions on the Ingletons' faces, which had now acquired a slight shade of green.

'It's a lie,' Luisa gasped. 'We were father's only children.'

'They are despicable creatures. Lowlifes. Imposters,' Philip chimed in.

'Oh.' Cassandra pulled an innocent face. 'You've completely misunderstood me. Actually, it's not what the Daily Telegraph wants to write about.'

'What do you mean?'

'The story they want to cover is the desecration of the grave of the prominent diplomat, your father, who put so much effort into the development of India and got robbed in the most egregious way. What was that you said about the imposters?'

'Where did you get this letter?' Philip tried to wrestle it out of the detective's hand, but she snatched it out of his grasp and stuffed it into her purse. No doubt, he would instantly recognize the forgery: Cassandra had added a few lines to make the writing sound more incriminating.

'From one of your father's friends. So will you be so kind as to answer a few questions about the late Mr Ingleton's diplomatic mission in India?' the detective asked as the trio brushed past her. 'It will help a lot with the investigation.'

'It is very unlikely!' Philip said. He maneuvered his sister into the vestibule, and butler Ogbourne slammed the door behind them.

'Well, they proved my theory.' Cassandra was beaming.

'How is that?' Valentine asked, taking the camera down from the tripod. 'They refused to talk.'

'On the contrary. They said all I needed to hear.'

CHAPTER 14

Strong Women and
Misplaced Brothers

It had been a week since Cassandra embarked on the Highgate case. Almost one hundred and seventy hours of building connections between the facts and witnesses, with no result in the hunt for the vandals. But there was a dead body on her conscience. That was what she had achieved.

That day passed in search of Omer Ingleton's illegitimate offspring. As it turned out, no one had ever heard of them, neither the National Census nor the family annals she had access to with the help of Omer Ingleton's secretary, who must have been a hundred years old. If there truly were any ghosts in this case, they were these evasive heirs.

Anyway, soon they would not even be her ghosts to hunt. Mr Redlaw had hired her for only seven days, and since the plundering of the graves was no longer the priority, in the morning he expressed his concern that a private detective in his house could compromise Scotland Yard's murder investigation. What he was really saying, of course, was his disappointed goodbye.

* * *

'Excuse me, madam, but you cannot smoke here,' said the owner of the tearoom, a neat woman with a note of hysteria in her voice. Cassandra stubbed her cigarette into the saucer with a half-finished cucumber sandwich – she did not care for an argument, nor for food.

She reached for some change in her purse and fished out a handful. Her mother's ring was sitting on top of the coins, catching the light of the setting sun reflected by the facade of the building across the street. That piece of jewellery was the only lead she had not yet looked into. How on earth did the perpetrators get hold of it? And what message were they trying to convey by tossing it to her feet? Perhaps, it was time she called home.

The nearest post office was just around the corner, so Cassandra trod down there, feeling every blister on her feet after a long day of paying visits and making inquiries. Alas, blisters were not the only thing that caused her discomfort; worse still was the prospect of the conversation with her family that she could postpone no further.

'Excuse me.' The detective squeezed past a boy who was wiping the glass doors of the post office with a rag, and entered the hall.

It was almost the end of the workday, but people still lined up with bundles and envelopes to be posted and sent out to all the corners of the world. Cassandra walked past the queue and peeked at the clerk through a small opening in the laced screen that separated customers from workers.

'Could I use the telephone?' she asked.

The clientele, all as one, studied her with curious looks: a rare home was fitted with a telephone, and those who could use one to connect with someone else ignited the interest of the telephoneless crowd.

'You could use our booth. We've only recently installed it.' The clerk, a jovial young woman, flashed a big-toothed smile at her, as if selling her on the newest service, and pointed at the booth to the right. 'It's two pennies. No time limit.'

'It won't take long,' Cassandra promised, very skeptical about the whole idea of making this call.

She left the payment on the counter, entered the booth and

closed the curtain, cutting off the curious stares of the other clients. There was a stool inside and a telephone mounted on the wooden wall. She stood and stared at the apparatus, reluctant, then picked up the earpiece and rotated the hand-crank.

'Number, please?' the female voice of the operator asked.

'Craster seven,' Cassandra said and sagged onto the stool, waiting for the operator to put her through.

The pause was long and impregnated with the quiet static of the working machine and her own anxious breathing.

'Caxton Hall, Grigg speaking,' a male voice introduced himself.

'Who the heck is Grigg?' Cassandra blurted out. 'Where is Tappington?'

'I am the new butler. Mr Tappington is no longer with us.'

'What do you mean no longer with us? Is he dead?'

'Is there anything I can help you with, madam?'

'My name is Cassandra Ayers and I'd like...'

'Ah, Lady Cassandra.' He articulated well because, probably, someone was standing right next to him, waiting for the call to be passed on to them.

'No one calls me that anymore. Just Miss Ayers, please.'

'How can I help you, Miss Ayers?'

'I'd like to talk to...' she sighed. 'To my father.'

'His Lordship is out.'

'Well, of course, he's out. Is he ever there when he's needed?'

'Would you like to leave a message?'

'Um. No, thank you, Grigg.'

'Cassandra?' the voice suddenly changed to female.

The detective squeezed her eyes shut. She had hoped she wouldn't have to talk to her stepmother, but there she was, on the other end of the line.

'Yes, Lydia. How... how are you?' The words awkwardly tumbled out of her mouth.

Silence stretched for a long moment.

'You haven't reached out to us for more than a year. We thought you were dead.'

'Wouldn't that simplify things?'

'You want to play a victim? How typical of you. Your father's been worried sick.'

'Oh, please. You both know my address. If he cared...'

'He went down with mumps. He didn't even make it to the Parliament session this year. What's wrong with you?' Lydia's half whisper hissed out of the receiver.

'Listen, I didn't call to fight.'

'Your father is an old man now. Whatever differences you had in the past...'

'Differences?' Cassandra couldn't believe the underestimation.

'You better make peace with him if you don't want to drive him to his grave.'

Something vile and toxic oozed out of the earpiece. That was exactly what had kept the detective away from home all these months. Lydia manipulated her into a state of guilt again: her old and sick father needed her filial love and attention.

'Everything your father did, he did for your own good. You were too young to understand.'

Her stepmother had resorted to that excuse over and over again for the past several years, the favourite excuse of all tyrants – they cause you pain for your own good. The real question was, what kind of father would break their child with the intention to make them whole?

'I...' her voice sounded weak in the storm of emotions that suddenly engulfed her – Lydia had finally achieved what she wanted. 'I will try to fix this, I promise.'

There was nothing to fix.

'But that's not why I'm calling. Er... has father been to the family crypt recently?'

'He goes there every week. You know that.' This fact annoyed Lydia. She couldn't stand the competition, even with the late wife of Joseph Ayers, Cassandra's father.

'Did he mention anything unusual?'

'Unusual? What do you mean?'

'Maybe someone broke into the crypt? Was anything stolen? Or maybe seemed off?'

'This conversation seems off. What happened?'

'Just answer the question, Lydia. Please.'

A loud and long sigh meant the woman was trying to remember.

'Nothing I can think of.'

Another dead end in the investigation.

'All right. I have to go now.'

'Although...' stepmother drawled.

'What?'

'He mentioned something about the door in the crypt or the lock. Something about it not working properly. I thought it was weird, since the door had been replaced not so long ago. Yes. I remember it clearly now. An artisan came from London. He brought the new stained-glass panes to fit into the crypt doors. A terrible creature. The reek of tobacco. Ugh. I had to keep the windows open for days.'

Cassandra's heart skipped a beat.

'Listen, Lydia. I know you never go there. But I need you to check one thing for me.'

The woman's sigh was again long and demanded some more pleading.

'What is it?'

'I need you to see if my mother is still wearing the ring.'

'Are you out of your mind? I'm not touching the corpse.'

It took a few minutes to talk her stepmother into fulfilling this request. The woman could not stand looking at the dead, but also, she always became useless whenever somebody needed her help. Finally, Cassandra promised to write to her father if Lydia did this for her. They agreed stepmother would send a telegram to the Redlaws' estate when she had checked the crypt. The conversation having drained her of all her vital power, the detective hung up the earpiece. She fixed her hair and hat, pulled the gloves on her shaky hands and left the booth.

As she stepped out of the post office, a gulp of fresh air

helped her soothe the anxiety that was slowly creeping up on her while Lydia's words about her failure as a daughter repeated in her head.

'Miss Ayers? Is that you?' A round and very fair face smiled at her from under the brim of a hat.

'Lucy?' She recognized Mrs Redlaw's maid. 'I'm sorry, I don't know your surname.'

'It's Miss Swan. So you *are* coming to the rally, after all?'

'The rally?' The detective frowned as she recalled the suffragettes' manifesto Lucy gave her a few days ago.

'Come on, Miss Ayers. It's in five minutes.'

The maid put her hand through Cassandra's and led her down the street. It wasn't part of the plan, but she complied. Anything seemed like a relief if it would postpone her packing her things to leave and talking with Mr Redlaw that night about her failed investigation.

They arrived at a bookstore decorated with banners and festoons of green, white and violet colours. A poster in the window showed a woman in armour wielding a sword. The caption above her read, "Vote for Women!" Below it said, "We fight to win!"

'I am not sure if this is my battle,' Cassandra said to Lucy. 'I'm not political.'

'Who says this is about politics?' The maid looked straight into her eyes. 'This is about freedom. You know how hard it is to get it. For some, it is nearly impossible. But you are brave and bright. You are fortunate to do what other women are dreaming about.'

Only someone who did not know anything about her life could call her fortunate. The thought made the detective snort, but the seriousness on Lucy's face didn't allow for any mockery.

'All right. Show me the way,' she said, giving in to pressure.

The maid, round and jolly as a bun, pushed the door open and led the way.

Inside, a little room was already crammed with people, mostly women, but a few men, too. An activist by the door took two rosettes with badges and ribbons out of her box and pinned them onto the chests of the two newcomers.

'Oh.' Cassandra did not expect the little poke into the lapel of her coat.

The room was densely populated with bookshelves, but the tiny space in the middle hosted an improvised rostrum facing a few rows of chairs. Some of the rally-goers talked to each other in confident voices; others, who had not yet decided how they felt about the event and ideas it promoted, stood aside, and glanced around sheepishly or paged through books.

Lucy found two seats uncomfortably close to the rostrum and the two landed there.

'I can't believe I'll meet *the* Emmeline Pankhurst,' she squeaked. 'She's a legend.'

'I'll give her that.' Cassandra wasn't so enthusiastic.

However, for the majority of conservative Londoners complacent about the status quo, Emmeline Pankhurst was just a nightmare that was going to destroy everything they cherished.

Being a self-made entrepreneur, Cassandra was weirdly reluctant to support the spread of this lifestyle. It almost felt like promoting the idea of going to war. Wasn't it simpler to follow the flow?

'Ladies and gentlemen, Mrs Pankhurst has just arrived,' the activist who distributed the badges by the door announced. 'We will begin shortly.'

Emmeline Pankhurst, a woman of forty-two, small and light like a feather, entered the room as though swept in by a draught, or maybe by a collective breath that rolled over the crowd. Feet shuffled towards the vacant seats as she smiled at her audience and took her place at the rostrum.

'Let me introduce our dearest guest.' The woman with the badges stood near the outstanding suffragette. 'She travelled all the way from Manchester to start a conversation we've been long awaiting. Please, welcome the one and only Emmeline Pankhurst.'

'Thank you, Effie. It's very sweet of you.' Mrs Pankhurst pulled out a long pin that held a big hat with violet flowers on her head, removed the hat and put it aside. No haste in either of her moves. The light of gas lamps fell onto her noticeably tired face. The woman fixed her hair and raised her eyes to the audience, who waited with bated breath while watching her. 'When coming here today, I was hesitant as to whether I wanted to talk about women's right to vote. You see, among other things, I occupy the position of Poor Law Guardian in Chorlton-on-Medlock. Just yesterday I was visiting a workhouse. There, I saw little girls, six or seven years old, on their knees, scrubbing the floors of the long corridors void of any humanity. I also saw a pregnant woman doing hard work right up until the moment she delivered a baby into this world, right where she was working. It appalled me. But what was still more appalling was that I had already seen this four years before, when I came to the workhouse for the first time. It meant nothing had changed since then. It meant I'd failed to make even the slightest change for those poor creatures. So I was coming here today burdened with my failure, and I didn't even know if I was entitled to talk to you. The right to vote,' she tut-tutted. 'Does it even matter whether we vote, if there are thousands dying within the walls of the workhouses in all corners of this country? Dying of hunger, of shame, of indifference? And then I thought, would it all be the same if women had their say in Parliament? If their word mattered in ruling this country? The answer is NO. Not a single female politician would allow a child to scrub cold cobbled floors and contract bronchitis. Not a single woman would turn a blind eye to the gruesome conditions encountered by a woman in labour in a workhouse. So if you ask me why the right to vote is so important for someone who doesn't even care about politics, I'll say, it is not about politics; it is about taking care of things our patriarchal society is indifferent to. Do you know what men can be and still not lose their right to vote? They can be drunkards, convicts, lunatics, unfit for service, slave owners. But a woman, even if she is a mayor, doctor, teacher or a mother, can't have a say. Why is that? What is there in our female nature that makes our opinion inferior to the one of a man who is a lunatic or a drunkard? I'll tell you what. It is in our female nature to care. And it is a very dangerous thing in politics, isn't it? To simply care.'

Had she even been breathing all this time? Cassandra didn't know. She quickly wiped off a tear that ran down her cheek, hoping that Lucy didn't see. Crying was a very private thing for her. As she raised her eyes, she saw Emmeline Pankhurst looking intently right at her in her moment of weakness, and hoped she wouldn't call her out for tearing up. Instead, Mrs Pankhurst just nodded as though she had achieved what she had hoped for.

'If there is at least one person here whom I've managed to persuade, I will consider this my victory,' the woman concluded.

'Oh. She is magnificent, isn't she?' Lucy piped and clapped vigorously together with the rest of the attendees. 'Brava!'

The audience sprang to their feet and the ovation grew more and more enthusiastic. Cassandra joined them. However feeble her legs were, she wanted to be standing for this.

After the speech, everyone enjoyed a bit of conversation with Mrs Pankhurst, who cruised the room and joined different groups of people. The woman with the badges, who turned out to be the owner of the bookstore, and her adolescent daughter offered the guests some scones and tea.

'I can't believe I'm going to talk to her,' Lucy said, crumbling a scone in her hands and munching nervously on the pieces of it.

'How did you learn about Mrs Pankhurst?' Cassandra asked.

'I...' it was obvious that she didn't want to talk about it.

'It's all right if you don't want to say, Miss Swan. It's none of my business.'

'I was in a workhouse.'

'You don't say.'

'Yes. I'm one of the women Mrs Pankhurst's organization helped out, although I've never met her in person. One of her dear friends took me to her home as a scullery maid and gave me good recommendations. That's how I got my place at the

Redlaws' estate. But...'

'I won't say a word, Lucy. I promise.'

'Thank you. It's not that I don't trust Mr and Mrs Redlaw. They're good people. But not everyone's like them.'

'Tell me about it,' Cassandra sipped her tea.

Emmeline Pankhurst shot an impatient glance at the detective while talking to the attendees just two steps away. She was obviously intrigued by Cassandra, for reasons known only to her. Finally, she exchanged goodbyes with the group and stepped towards Lucy and her curious companion.

'Oh, Mrs Pankhurst!' the maid gasped. 'I'm honoured.'

'Nonsense,' the woman swatted her hand at the words. 'What's your name, dear?'

'Lucy Swan. You probably don't know me, but I know you. I once was in a workhouse in Manchester. Your friend, Mrs Boyle, took me as a scullery maid. I'm forever grateful.'

'My dear girl.' Mrs Pankhurst gave a hearty squeeze to the girl's hand.

'Oh. And this is Miss Ayers,' Lucy quickly added.

'Cassandra.' The detective reached out for a handshake.

'*The* Cassandra Ayers?'

'You know me?'

'I believe it was you who got my friend out of a terrible pickle. A case of a banshee terrorizing a remote village out of Manchester.'

That was a case she remembered very well. A woman had been persecuted by the villagers for witchcraft, but she was simply gathering herbs and making concoctions.

'Mertie Coldbridge is your friend?' she asked.

'Yes. She showed me your portrait in the local newspaper,' Mrs Pankhurst explained. 'I cut it out for my collection of women who make a difference.'

'I didn't know I was in anyone's collection.'

'Oh, yes. You are.' She took a cup of tea from the tray.

'It's nothing in comparison to what you are doing,' Cassandra said. 'To be honest, I expected something different from this meeting.'

'I know. You expected a lot of screaming and wringing hands? Denying love and marriage? Brandishing swords, or, rather, kitchen knives?' Mrs Pankhurst chuckled. 'Trust me, there are more combative gatherings than this one. But it requires a different level of... anger and desperation, which becomes tiring very fast.'

The three women exchanged a reserved smile over their teacups.

'I was wondering,' Cassandra started, 'how I could help the cause.'

'But you are already helping. You are using your education and common sense, which is rather rare, I should tell you, to help people, to guide them out of their debilitating stupidity. Just continue defending what you believe in, and that will be a model that will encourage other women to follow in your footsteps.'

'I'm seriously not sure anyone would want to follow in my footsteps. My life... well, in a nutshell, it's been...' the detective was trying to find the proper words, when suddenly Mrs Pankhurst put her warm and comforting hand on her arm.

'There is nothing shameful in hurting,' she said, looking right in Cassandra's eye. 'The pain we've endured is what helps us understand the sufferings of others. Pain is the best educator. Be proud of yours.'

The woman took out a calling card and extended it to the detective.

'Call on me if you ever feel like it. It was nice meeting both of you.' She smiled and moved on to the next group.

Cassandra looked at the piece of paper in her hands and traced its rugged texture with her thumb while contemplating the conversation she had just had.

'I can't believe it.' The maid's whisper was ecstatic. 'I feel so privileged to even stand between you and Mrs Pankhurst, two educated women who've built their careers. This is phenomenal. If you think about it, there are so many strong and kind-natured women around us all the time. Take Mrs Redlaw. She always gives out free meals on Christmas. Last year she sponsored the burial of a former groundsman who had no family or means. Or take Miss Tesmond. She's been through a lot. She singlehandedly takes care of her brother. Brings him food every week, treats his gout. Poor thing can't afford a doctor. He returned from India last Christmas. That's what she said. Returned penniless.'

Lucy's words prompted something to occur to Cassandra, and she stared into the void, dumbstruck.

CHAPTER 15

The Séance of Hypnosis

Mrs Redlaw scurried into the reception room carrying a vase full of flowers. She put it on the table and supervised Lucy as the latter arranged the candles. The mistress's double chin bobbed as she nodded her approval. Since Cassandra asked her to organize this evening in aid of the investigation, this was the only thing the woman could think of.

'You sure, Miss Ayers, this will help you solve the case?' the superintendent asked as he watched his busy wife.

'Absolutely. In fact, I've already solved it in my head. I'm only sorry it took me so long.' The detective sauntered into the room, slightly worried in anticipation of the evening.

'Oh? Why don't you just share with me what you know?'

'Unfortunately, I don't have any proof of my guess, only my assumptions. I'm hoping I'll expose the perpetrator and force them to make a confession.'

'You don't want to say the person who did this, who,' he whispered, 'murdered Gummidge, is one of us?'

Cassandra gave him a meaningful stare.

'Good grief,' Mr Redlaw said quietly. 'Tell me who it is.'

'You'll know everything by the end of this night.'

'But isn't it too dangerous having this person here?'

'I'm afraid this person has been under this roof for too long already.'

'Don't you worry, my dearest Cassie.' Mrs Redlaw reappeared

in the room with an ever more luxuriant bouquet of flowers. She started stuffing them into the vases on the mantle. 'Everything will be splendid tonight.'

The guests started arriving at six o'clock, all on time, to the hostess's satisfaction. It was, of course, a reserved satisfaction, because of poor Reverend Gummidge. Her every laugh ended with a sigh, her voice went from dramatic soprano to contralto, and she had tied a black ribbon around her upper arm.

'He was such a nice person,' Mr Redlaw repeated, with an expression as though speaking of a martyred saint.

Those present – Cassandra, Mr Redlaw, Miss Tesmond, Lavinia, William Drummond and Valentine – responded with respectful silence.

After dinner, to enjoy some parlour games, the guests moved into the music room, where a grand piano stood in the middle of the room. But charades were frowned upon as it was too jolly, considering the circumstances. Mrs Redlaw suggested a round of cards.

'Cards. What a frivolous game.' William Drummond smoothed his moustache with an index finger and thumb. The superintendent's wife became flustered.

'In Willy's regiment, they cracked down on gambling,' Lavinia explained. 'Cards are prohibited for now.'

'Didn't know they have morals in the army,' Valentine mumbled into his glass of port. Only Cassandra, seated beside him, noticed his remark, but was too distracted by the anticipation of what this evening might bring.

'Well, we are not in the regiment, are we?' Mrs Redlaw sat down, pouting.

'I prefer Backgammon,' Drummond went on.

'Willy is very good at it.' Lavinia took her place behind the armchair where he sat, her hands resting on his shoulders.

Cassandra would have rolled her eyes but kept her emotions in check. This evening, after all, was not about Lavinia and her husband. Apparently, some barely perceptive tremble of her facial muscles made her stifled impulse obvious to Drummond.

'And you, Miss Ayers, do you have a hobby to share with us?' he asked. 'Perhaps you make voodoo dolls?'

The detective puffed out smoke in his direction.

'You'd be the first to know,' she said.

His face dropped. Valentine laughed but disguised it as a choking cough.

'We sometimes play croquet,' Mrs Redlaw said in a low voice, as if to herself, and sighed. 'Reverend Gummidge would join us, poor thing.'

'I like draughts,' Miss Tesmond said. 'My brother taught me how to play. In fact, it was our only entertainment during long nights at my aunt's home after my mother passed away.'

'Your brother who's in India now?' Cassandra recalled.

'Yes. That's right.'

Now, with the picture already complete in the detective's mind, every word had a different ring to it.

'How is the *investigation* progressing, Miss Ayers?' Drummond asked, making the word *investigation* sound particularly ludicrous.

'Let's not go there.' Mr Redlaw tapped one finger on a glass of whiskey, which looked a little fuller than what he usually drank.

'I'm simply curious,' the captain shrugged. 'The *detective* has been here for more than a week now. Are there any results? Or is she merely waiting for the gruesome scenario to further unfold?'

'Captain,' the superintendent warned him.

'If you want my opinion, it's a business the police should take care of, not some amateur with wild fantasies,' was Drummond's conclusion.

Valentine shot a glance at Cassandra, checking if she was on the brink of retaliating. When he saw that she was still going to ignore the prickly comments, he said, 'Miss Ayers has been building her case all this time. This is not something settled over the course of a single evening.'

'Of course not.' A smirk curled one corner of the captain's

mouth. 'Especially if the detective is...'

'Music,' Mrs Redlaw suddenly exclaimed and sprang to her feet. 'Lavinia, darling, why don't you play for us?'

'As a matter of fact, I've got a hobby I can share with you,' Cassandra responded with a delay. 'Why not? I'd like you all to participate in a little experiment.' She pulled at her cigarette until there wasn't any room for air in her lungs.

'Oh?' The hostess sagged back onto the ottoman.

'Don't let the experimental nature of it fool you. It's rather effective.'

'So what is it?' the hostess was dying to know.

'Hypnosis.'

Mrs Redlaw looked as if a bomb had exploded over her head.

'Oh, Cassie, you must show us!'

'That's preposterous,' Drummond snorted.

'In fact, many inspectors are already using this method,' Cassandra reassured them.

'That's true,' Valentine chimed in. 'I've read about this in the newspapers. Apparently, it's a thing now.'

'Even if it works, shouldn't it be a Doctor of Medicine who performs it?' was Lavinia's weak protest.

'Exactly,' her husband agreed. 'Well done, darling.'

'I learnt from the best, *the* Dr Bentzel, after I underwent treatment at his clinic Lavinia was so kind to mention at our last dinner,' Cassandra said. Her friend pursed her lips. The memories of Dr Bentzel's hideous maniacal face made the detective shudder. 'I'm also learning more from Émile Coué and Pierre Janet's books. Right now I can apply hypnosis and make a breakthrough in the investigation. If, of course, someone volunteers to help me. Someone who has seen the ghost.'

Everyone stared at Miss Tesmond.

'Me?' The secretary's eyebrows arched over her glasses.

'Miss Tesmond, would you be kind enough to assist me?' The detective tapped her cigarette into an ashtray and put her chair opposite the sofa where Miss Tesmond was sitting. She sat down opposite the secretary, so close that the woman nervously shifted her position and looked around for someone to save her from this.

Mr Redlaw, who had started gathering what was about to happen, became more visibly tense. Everyone became more alert. Even skeptical Captain Drummond leaned forward.

'I'll explain everything to you, ladies and gentlemen,' Cassandra started. 'In the Middle Ages, there was an outbreak of dancing plague. Thousands of people would dance days on end, until they collapsed, exhausted or dead. The phenomenon is yet unknown to science. According to different theories, people who engaged in mass dancing were either poisoned or suffered from frustration caused by plagues, famine, floods and other natural disasters. All that matters in our story is the fact that people can fall victim to mass hysteria. What else would explain why all the groundsmen collectively succumbed to the belief they were dealing with a ghost at the cemetery? But after speaking with all of them, I learnt that only two people actually saw the ghost: Ellie Tesmond and Ed Brockington.'

'You don't think that I am a victim of mass hysteria?' The secretary looked around in search of support. 'Because I saw it. With my own eyes. I told you.'

'Of course!' Cassandra reassured her with a brief smile. 'That's what I thought. Why would you lie about the encounter? And I trust you. I think you were tricked into believing you saw something. In fact, you are the only person here who can help solve this case.'

'I am?'

'You were sleepwalking when you saw the ghost. It is extremely likely that under hypnosis you may recall more details about that night.'

'How extraordinary!' Mrs Redlaw regained her dramatic soprano.

'Is this even legal?' William Drummond asked, but everyone ignored him.

The prospect of what was about to happen made Miss Tesmond fidget uneasily.

'I don't know,' she said, her eyebrows knit together.

'I can't mesmerize you against your will, Miss Tesmond. And when I do, you will be in total control, so there is nothing to be afraid of.'

'Come on, Ellie! Don't be such a chicken! If only I had seen the ghost!' Mrs Redlaw pursed her lips, disappointed in herself.

'All right, then,' Miss Tesmond agreed.

'Capital!' Mrs Redlaw sat closer and put her glass aside.

'Well, this is absurd!' Drummond sprang to his feet with a squeak of his leather boots. 'You will let this charlatan –'

'Easy, Captain!' Mr Redlaw raised a protective palm like the gesture of a fun-fair magician, returning the man into his armchair.

Cassandra sat with her back to Drummond, but she could feel the man's hateful glare burning a hole in the nape of her neck.

'Now, everyone must keep quiet,' she commanded.

Mrs Redlaw covered her mouth with a hand.

The detective started tapping her stick rhythmically against the floor, and when she spoke, her voice was low-pitched and monotonous.

'Breathe deeply. Listen to my voice. You are completely calm.'

With her hands in her lap, Miss Tesmond sat completely upright. Her eyes shut. Her deep breathing entwined with the crackling of the fire.

'Return to that night,' Cassandra said, tapping her stick on the parquet. 'You are walking down the lane at the cemetery. The night is silent, except for the sound of the owls hooting. You hear whimpering. You open your eyes. What do you see?'

'I see Berta Everett's gravestone,' Miss Tesmond answered in a strange somnambular voice.

Mrs Redlaw clasped two hands to her mouth now, her eyes popping with astonishment. Her husband, who had been sitting with his legs crossed, swirling the whiskey in his glass with a skeptical attitude, leaned forward.

'I hear a sad wailing. I turn around. I see a white figure by the entrance to the Egyptian Avenue.'

'Is it a man or a woman?' Cassandra asked.

The secretary squinted her eyes as if trying to see.

'I can't say. There's a halo around it.'

'What is it doing?'

'It's just hovering there and looking at me. Through me.'

'Do you see anything else?'

Suddenly, the mesmerized woman grabbed the armrest of the sofa. Lavinia quietly gasped.

'I see them! The ghost points at them! They are digging out the grave!'

'Who are they?'

'A man and a woman.'

'Have you ever seen them before?'

'No.'

'Can you describe them?'

The secretary took a moment. The tension in the room swelled to the extent it could shatter the walls. A sudden knock on the entrance door made everyone jump. The ties drawing them to Miss Tesmond broke. But Cassandra's eyes were still trained on the secretary who had woken up from the hypnosis and seemed surprised to see the long faces goggling at her.

'Have I helped you?' Her voice was normal again.

'Most certainly.' Cassandra rose.

'But what does it mean?' the superintendent asked.

'I'll explain in a moment.'

The Redlaw's butler entered the room.

'There is a man outside claiming that he has a very urgent matter with Miss Ayers.'

'Curiouser and curiouser,' Cassandra intoned as she stepped into the hall, where she encountered an elderly man whose white tresses usually covering the bald patch on his head like a veil were now in disarray, as if he had been dragged through bushes. This was a new, less impeccable version of the Ingleton's butler, Ogbourne.

'What happened?' the detective asked.

'You must come – quick!' In his hands the man was holding a brush he must have been using and which he'd forgotten to let go of in his haste to leave the house. 'Mr Ingleton... he... he has been arrested! But he did nothing wrong! It was the other two!'

No further explanations were needed. Cassandra grabbed her coat and her stick and jumped into the waiting carriage. Ogbourne leapt up with the coachman, who whipped up the horses, and they sped off at breakneck speed.

CHAPTER 16

The Spade in the Storeroom

T he journey to Arlington Street from the superintendent's estate would normally take more than thirty minutes, but the horses dashed at a dangerous pace through dark London, where fog mixed with smoke and hung over the city like an impenetrable curtain.

Cassandra reclined in the corner of the cab; darkness obscured her face. Only the tip of her nose and peaks of her cheekbones were exposed to the dim light of the gas streetlamps, inquisitively peeking now and then into the cab.

The gears of her thoughts were in motion, revolving and propelling the pictures of events as she imagined them, like Muybridge's *Horse in Motion* – an illusion of movement created by means of rapidly changing still pictures. An illusion. That's what happened in the Highgate case, too: everyone was made to believe in an illusion.

The carriage hurtled past a cluster of people forming a merry queue before the entry of Madam Tussaud's. In their eagerness to see the legendary figurines, they didn't notice and didn't care how the wheels of cabs and carriages were splashing water from the road onto their clothes: the spectacle distracted them from the problem. At the cemetery as well, everyone had been so thrilled by the stories of the ghost, they didn't see what was really happening; in fact, they would be disappointed to know what an absolutely quotidian business all of it had been.

When they arrived at Ingleton's house, the housekeeper was standing at the porch with a lantern, like a sailor's wife guiding her husband out of a storm at sea.

'She is very bad,' the housekeeper said, nodding into the depths of the house.

Very bad wasn't an exaggeration. Luisa Carstone was sitting at the edge of a chair, ashen-faced, her fists clutched to her chest, like Mary, Queen of Scots, before her execution.

Cassandra set an uncomfortable stool in front of Luisa and sat down, leaning on her cane.

'Now, Mrs Carstone, tell me what happened.'

'I... I... they...' she made a few more attempts before her jaws stopped obeying her, and her mouth produced only indistinct gibberish.

The detective readdressed the questioning look to the butler.

'The police searched the house,' he answered. 'They found a spade in our gardener's storeroom, stained with blood.'

'Why did they search the house in the first place?'

'They said they'd been informed.'

'And they had a warrant?'

'They did.' Ogbourne's eyes were tragically downcast, then he noticed the water was dripping from his clothes onto the carpet and stepped hurriedly onto the parquet, even now obeying his practical reasoning.

The detective looked at Luisa Carstone, who only yesterday would not have hesitated to crush her, Cassandra, like some sort of despicable insect. A moment of triumph at seeing her laid low came and passed. She gripped Luisa firmly by her hand.

'Now, Mrs Carstone, you will tell me everything about your half-siblings.'

Only more inarticulate whimpering came out of Luisa's contorted mouth.

'If you don't speak, your brother will be hanged.'

That was like a sobering slap in her face. Luisa swallowed, blinked and stared at Cassandra.

'When did you find out that your father had other children?'

'Two years ago they wrote to us for the first time, claiming to be the children of our father, by way of a woman he met on the continent. According to them, she became his wife after my mother died. But they had no proof, none. They claimed it was destroyed in a house fire about five years ago. How convenient. We didn't believe them.'

'And so they tried to extort money from you?'

Luisa nodded.

'You refused them?'

'Of course, we refused them! Those vagabonds didn't receive a penny from us!'

'And they started blackmailing you?'

'Yes. They terrorized us. Sent a letter every day or even twice a day. But then suddenly it stopped. They gave up.'

'No, I don't think they did. They just found another way.'

'What do you mean?'

Cassandra explained that the blackmailers had somehow sniffed out the information about the Order their father had belonged to, and about the mythical treasure the Order allegedly hid, most likely in the graves of their former members. Armed with that information, they had started their search with their father's grave, and then went on to the others.

'What monster would do such a thing?' asked the housekeeper.

'Do you have the letters?' the detective asked.

'No, Philip and I burnt all of them.'

'And you never reported the blackmail to the police?'

Luisa turned away, annoyed with Cassandra's pragmatism, which obviously meant *no*.

'Do you at least know their names?'

'Oh, yes. They called themselves Rose and Fredrick Wharton.'

'A sister and brother, then.' Cassandra was thinking aloud as her suspicion was proved.

'We made inquiries,' the woman went on. 'We know that Rose Wharton was an actress in some third-rate theatre. As for him, he'd spent six years in India, serving in the British Army.'

'Why wouldn't you just tell me all this when I first came here?' Cassandra sighed. 'If you had, you wouldn't be in the pickle you are now in. But most importantly, a man's life could've been saved.'

'Oh, save your preaching for somebody else,' Luisa glared at her with the airs of an insulted queen. 'So what about my brother? Will you get him out of prison?'

The temptation to say "no" was rather strong. But of course, such a small delight was not worth a noose around Philip Ingleton's neck, no matter how badly that neck required a good slap.

'I might help him, but I'll charge you twice my usual price. Twenty pounds plus any additional expenses.'

'So that's what you do? Fleece people when they are most vulnerable?'

'Thirty pounds,' Cassandra corrected herself. 'Think twice, Mrs Carstone, for every next word may cost you another ten pounds.'

Luisa bit her tongue. The detective walked out the door and left the woman bloating like a toad. She smiled to herself. Now the puzzle was complete.

CHAPTER 17

An American Contraption

Little had changed in the music room in the superintendent's house since Cassandra's abrupt departure. The company was still assembled, listening silently as Lavinia played the piano. They all shook off their drowsiness as soon as the detective reappeared in the room.

'We decided to wait for you, Cassie,' Mrs Redlaw said. 'We were worried about you.'

'You were abducted by a stranger.' Her husband came up to the bar cart. 'Would you care for some wine?'

Cassandra was pleased to see her cigarette case on the table.

'A glass of whiskey would do better, thank you,' she answered, as she adjusted a cigarette into the holder.

William Drummond snorted, unfolded himself from the armchair and walked around the room, the leather of his boots creaking.

'You ride at night with men, you smoke, you drink whiskey,' he spat. 'Mr Redlaw, are you sure your wife's reputation is safe near this woman?' He pointed at Cassandra.

'William, really,' Lavinia protested.

'I'm sure of only one thing, Captain,' the superintendent said, passing a glass of whiskey to Cassandra, 'and that is that you and I are not progressive enough. We are men of the past. And Miss Ayers is a woman of the future.' He encouraged her with a smile, while himself he encouraged with a gulp of whiskey, an action his wife frowned upon.

'Easy, my dear,' she patted his arm. 'Don't forget that I'm a chairwoman of the Sobriety Association.'

'Well, luckily, I'm not.'

'So where did you go, Miss Ayers?' Valentine asked. 'As your partner, shouldn't I have accompanied you?'

With a sip of whiskey, the detective tried to scorch out the unpleasant anticipation that stirred in her gut, but it didn't go away. She then raised a cigarette to her lips, brought it to life with a series of deep pulls and put out the match by giving it a shake in the air. The match died, emitting a thin wisp of smoke that curled around Cassandra's face in the shape of a question mark. Everyone watched this ritual.

'You know, most people are afraid of cemeteries,' she said. 'It's not difficult, at all, to nourish this innate, ancient fear. A gossip mentioned in passing, or a practical joke, like grabbing someone in the dark, can make one watch for their own shadow their entire life. Gripped by hysteria, people can even start experiencing hallucinations. They can even genuinely believe they've seen or heard something out of this world. Mind games. Fascinating how our brains can play such tricks on us.'

Outside it started to rain in earnest; heavy drops sounded like thousands of tiny fists knocking insistently on the window.

'I wondered why anyone would need to play such a horrid trick that would make people leave their jobs. The reason is very simple – someone needed the cemetery deserted, fewer eyes watching it, less attention. Unattended, it was an easier target for a plunderer searching for treasure.'

Mrs Redlaw sent her husband an I-told-you-so look.

'The treasure, which, supposedly, has been hidden by the Order of Holy Protectors, and which the plunderer believes is buried in a grave with one of the Order's members.'

'Believes?' the superintendent's wife asked. 'So it wasn't poor Reverend Gummidge?'

'Reverend Gummidge's only sin was greed. I asked him about

the Order and the treasure. He put two and two together, waited 'till night, and set out for a treasure hunt himself. Only he found no valuables, just his own death, at the hands of people who would stop at nothing.'

'Perhaps from the man and woman I saw at the cemetery?' Miss Tesmond asked, a reflection of flames from the fire dancing in her glasses.

Cassandra's long gaze made her avert her eyes. The detective's cigarette was almost down to the nub, so she put it out in the ashtray and sloshed more whiskey into the glass, to a disdainful snort from Captain Drummond.

'Miss Tesmond is a witness. She saw the ghost. Or not? The hardest thing for me was to understand why she would need to stick to this lie. Was she naive, prompted by someone, or did she have her own agenda?'

'But I saw it! I saw it with my own eyes!' the secretary protested.

'With all due respect, Miss Tesmond, you couldn't see it because you are as blind as a bat. I do not suppose you sleepwalk in your glasses. From the distance you claim to be from the Egyptian Avenue that night, you couldn't have seen it.'

'Why would I lie about it?' Miss Tesmond's eyes were wide open, innocent, like daisies.

'For the same reason you lied that you saw the ghost pointing at a man and a woman.'

'What do you mean? How could I lie if I was hypnotized?'

'But you were not. I didn't hypnotize you because I have no such skill. I only pretended, to confirm you had been lying all this time. All you said during the séance you made up.'

Mrs Redlaw gasped.

'Good Lord.' Her husband squeezed his eyes shut, starting to guess what the detective was driving at.

'You mentioned a man and a woman digging out the grave to simply frame Philip Ingleton and Luisa Carstone. You knew that your brother had planted evidence in their house – a spade covered in blood. The blood of poor foolish Reverend Gummidge.

It was either you or your brother who killed the man when he walked up to you digging out the grave.'

The mouths of everyone in the room gaped open.

'Your real name is Rose Wharton. And your brother is Ed Brockington, also known as Fredrick Wharton. You two were good. But not good enough with the detail and nuance. Ed Brockington, a supposed gardener, but a gardener who does not take care of his own garden. While I was at his house, I noticed a neat basket with food, which only could have been brought by a loving woman, but Ed Brockington is no catch for any woman. But a sister? A sister would take care of her own brother. You also made a mistake. You mentioned in passing that your brother was in India; however, yesterday Lucy shared with me that your brother had returned.'

'And your aunt you have been visiting... it wasn't an aunt?' Mrs Redlaw put in.

'The night Reverend Gummidge was murdered, I found a cigar stub in the crypt,' Cassandra went on. 'That was a perfect hiding place that Fredrick used.'

'This is a terrible misunderstanding,' Miss Tesmond said, blinking. 'I don't know what she's talking about.'

'The performance is over, Rose,' Cassandra said. 'It's over.'

Miss Tesmond dropped her insecure manner. The brittle little woman they had known gave way to what she really was – a daring and artful swindler.

'You are right, it's over. It was getting very tiresome.' Even her voice was different now – low-pitched and a little husky.

Rose sprang to her feet, a revolver in her hand, aiming it at Cassandra. Mrs Redlaw and Lavinia shrieked. William Drummond covered half of the reception room in one stride to shield his wife with his body. Valentine froze. Mr Redlaw shifted from one foot to the other in uncertainty.

Cassandra calmly finished her whiskey and put the glass down.

'You think you are so clever, don't you?' The fake secretary bared her teeth like a snake.

'Most of the time, yes, I think I am.'

'And what will you do now?'

Rose cocked the hammer of the revolver. Mrs Redlaw produced an ear-piercing shriek of phenomenal length.

'Is everything all right, madam?' Stubbs peeked into the reception room and turned to a pillar of salt at seeing a gun in the secretary's hand.

His interference distracted Rose for a moment, and it was enough for the detective. She raised her cane and aimed it at the perpetrator like a gun.

It was three years ago when Cassandra ordered her cane with a secret from an American gunsmith, who dexterously hid firearms in lighters, fans, musical instruments and even combs for civilians who wanted to protect themselves by carrying a concealed weapon wherever they went – quite an asset in wild America. For a woman in her trade, it had been a lifesaver on several occasions. Its only disadvantage – it had just one round. There would be no second chances.

Cassandra lingered. She didn't want to shoot, but she saw a minute twitch of Rose's finger on the trigger. She was going to pull it. A resonant clap rang out.

A very long moment snailed by. No one moved, as if playing freeze game. Their faces contorted into masks of horror. Cassandra's heart was leaping. It seemed to her she had missed, but then Rose flopped onto the sofa, staring at the bloody flower that started to blossom on her shoulder.

'You shot me,' she whispered in astonishment.

* * *

Two constables carried Rose Wharton on the stretcher to the motorized ambulance. Pale and immobilized, the woman stared at the company of people who stood on the porch and watched the scene in absolute bewilderment.

The policemen hopped into the wagon and shut the doors. The subdued party stayed put on the porch of the house, their eyes still trained on the vehicle as it sped out of the yard.

'I'm sorry it ended like this,' Cassandra said, either to herself or to anyone listening.

'What a nasty creature,' William Drummond spat. 'She had it coming.'

Mrs Redlaw looked at him from under her curly bangs, for the first time speechless.

'Let's go inside. The ladies will get cold.' Mr Redlaw threw an arm around his wife's shoulders and pulled her close, a little more stooping under the burden of what had happened.

As everyone entered the house, Drummond grabbed the detective rather unceremoniously by her arm.

'Hey,' Valentine protested and stepped towards the captain.

'It's all right, Mr Duvar,' Cassandra reassured him, smiling calmly despite the pain the man's fingers caused her, digging into her flesh.

'I'm warning you,' Drummond whispered. 'I will not tolerate you around my wife. You are not fit for polite company. And I will not allow you to be a bad influence on her. My God, you shoot people for payment.'

Cassandra held his glare with her eyes, not blinking. Then one by one she unbent his fingers, releasing her arm.

'Yes, Captain Drummond, sometimes I shoot people for payment. But remember this: I would shoot *you* for free.'

* * *

The next morning, bright sunlight cleared the fog from the cemetery's alleys, but it was the deceitful sun of late autumn – devoid of any warmth. Frost solidified the mud and starched the foliage. The cold wind wrapped its fingers around Cassandra's neck and bit at her ears. She rubbed her lobes when strolling around the cemetery with Mr Redlaw.

'So the ghost doesn't exist?' he asked.

'No. Only in the stories of Rose and Fredrick Wharton. They wanted to intimidate your workers, and they certainly achieved their aim.'

'And what about the whimpering the workers heard?'

'Ah, the whimpering of a woman. Rose Wharton used to be an actress. I bet she can disguise her voice in many ways.

Together with her brother, she made sure the cemetery emptied out.'

'It all sounds like a very clever scheme.'

'It does. Miss Wharton is quite resourceful. If they ever find Fredrick, I think he will confirm that Rose was the brains of their plot. She spent a lot of time studying the cemetery, making sketches of the symbols from the graves, telling everyone that it was her hobby. In fact, she was looking for graves with the coat of arms of the Order engraved on them. That's why she didn't want to show me the album.'

'It's a shame the police didn't catch her brother,' Mr Redlaw said, squinting at the bright sun.

A red-bearded man passed by, pushing a wheelbarrow loaded with foliage so heavy it furrowed the ground. He tipped his hat at his employer and the detective.

'You've hired a new groundsman?' Cassandra asked.

The man stole a glance at her from under the peak of his woolen flat cap.

'Yes. The cemetery needs to be looked after. But it seems they've started with the Terrace Catacombs, though I told them to begin with the main path.' Mr Redlaw pursed his lips into a thin line. 'The workers don't mind my orders anymore. I think I'm losing my grip.'

They stopped before Omer Ingleton's grave, which had been returned to its former state. They stood there for a while in silence, until Mr Redlaw sighed with nostalgia and said, 'It might sound strange, but I will miss all this mysterious gothic charm. Do you really believe, Miss Ayers, that there is nothing beyond our understanding in this world, and that the dead cannot communicate with us?'

In the pocket of her coat, Cassandra fumbled with her mother's ring.

'I'm afraid, all the dead are dead for good. And not a single one wants to roam this bleak and wintry world.'

'Well, it was a pleasure having you here, Miss Ayers.' The superintendent reached out for a handshake.

'May I ask you for one last favour?'

'Anything.'

'Harmon Dilworth, the boy who used to work here before all this havoc.'

'What about him?'

'When I paid him a visit, he and his mother came across as decent people. I'm sure he'd be happy to be restored to his job at the cemetery. But he's too shy to ask for it himself.'

For a moment, the superintendent was surprised, or even taken aback. He sure wasn't used to asking his former employees to do him honour and return to his employ if they had handed in their notice themselves. A struggle between the usual upper-class snobbery and his better self showed on the man's face.

'Of course, Miss Ayers,' he finally said. 'I'll write him a letter.'

They resumed their stroll, shuffling along the foliage-coated alley bathed in sunlight.

CHAPTER 18

Our House Has Very Narrow Beds

The telegram from Lydia was brief. *Someone broke into the crypt. The ring is not there. Keep your promise.* No word was spared for affection. Although it was all words typed by a machine, Cassandra could hear the plummy voice of her stepmother in every letter of the last sentence.

However, the moment was not right for dwelling on family squabbles, so the detective prioritized the other fact: the ring that had been obviously stolen from the crypt. She made a mental note about it when sitting in the reception area at Newgate Prison, where all awaiting trial were detained, including Rose Wharton. Cassandra had come to ask her about her brother, Fredrick Wharton, who was still missing. Did she hope for any help from Rose? No. Not at all.

'You can see her now,' a stout woman in a black robe announced to Cassandra, before walking away to the accompaniment of jingling keys on a chain.

The detective followed her into the adjacent hallway where there was no longer any noise from the clerks typing letters, nor from the shuffling feet of the constables and wardens who came in and walked out in the performance of their business. In this hallway, the silence of the three-foot-thick walls and metal doors was more arresting than any shackles would ever be. Cassandra's pace slowed down as she took in the inhumane side of justice.

'Well, don't stand there gawking,' the jailer croaked. 'I sure have more important things to do than chaperone you around, Miss.'

Her meaty hand waved at the open door. The visitor approached. Inside, Rose sat at a table, pallid and bandaged. Cassandra entered, and the door immediately closed behind her with a resounding thud. The imprisoned woman and the detective stared at each other for a very long moment.

'I see you've been treated kindly,' Rose said, nodding in the direction of the jailor, who watched them through the peep window. 'Those on this side of the bars get batons instead of words.'

'It is a matter of our own choice which side of the bars we are on,' Cassandra answered. 'We all have a personal constable following us every day and preventing us from going astray – our moral principles. As far as I can judge, you have none.'

Rose burst into laughter.

'Moral principles. That's a reach for someone like you.'

'Someone like me? And what would that be?'

'Someone who'd shoot a person.'

'Weren't you going to do the exact same thing?'

'I was doing it to survive. What was your purpose? To establish the truth? You selfish cow. You can't possibly understand what someone like me goes through.'

'All right. Explain it to me, then.' Cassandra pushed a chair closer to the table and sat across from her.

'I won't explain shit to you.'

'Think twice. Maybe I'm your last opportunity in the foreseeable future to talk to someone more intelligent than that charming lady who waits outside the room.'

As she considered this, Rose munched on some air in her mouth.

'Come on, Rose. I know you want your story to be heard.'

'What's the point? No one ever listens in this God-forsaken city.'

'I am listening.'

'All right. But I'm not doing it for you. I'm doing it for Mr and Mrs Redlaw. They were kind to me. I'm sorry it all turned out like this. I hope if they know the truth, they won't judge me so harshly.'

She wrapped herself tightly into a grey prison-issued shawl. Colours that would hint at any joy were exiled from Newgate. Not only was the shawl devoid of lively colour, but it also wasn't enough to protect anyone trapped here from the slightest draught or bleakness of life.

'Have you got a cigarette?' Rose asked.

Cassandra took out her cigarette case and offered it to the woman. The inmate raised a cigarette to her lips and stashed the rest of the case contents under her robe.

'You owe me this,' she said.

'So you wanted me to say something to Mr and Mrs Redlaw? Go on, then.'

Rose's thin lips pulled hungrily at the cigarette.

'I didn't want to kill the reverend. Fredrick didn't want to either. It just happened.'

'Because you value money over a man's life.'

'Screw you. You don't know how it is to be born in the slums and be raised in hell.'

'You might be surprised.'

'Fredrick and I had a third sibling, a little girl named Julia. She died. It was the day before Christmas when coppers threw us out of our home. My father was very much dead by then, so we no longer received any money from him. Mother sold some of the jewellery he'd given her. That's what we'd lived on until that Christmas. We had nowhere to go so we ended up homeless. The scariest thing was my first night in the streets. It's so weird, don't you think, how much we trust that the four walls we call home will protect us from everything? But when the walls are gone, nothing stops the world from tearing you apart. And it did. Oh, yes, it did. In the morning, we found Julia dead. She had frozen to death. I'll never forget how they sang Christmas carols everywhere, how light twinkled in well-to-do homes, how everyone celebrated the birth of the all-loving God. But love and charity weren't for everyone. Soon, my mother had to prostitute herself for food. As for Fredrick and me, we started stealing, from pockets, in the markets, anywhere we could. In a year, mother was admitted to Bedlam. She died there from syphilis. The rest is history.' She stopped and stared at the glowing cigarette. 'Do you think they'll hang me?'

'I won't lie. Your situation is dire. If only it wasn't you who killed the reverend...'

'If you think I'll snitch on my brother...'

'I don't think anything, Rose. I'm just telling you the facts. You might win a reduction in your sentence if you co-operate with the police and lead them to your brother. I don't believe it was you who beat Gummidge to death with a spade.'

'You're a funny little thing, Miss Ayers. First you get me arrested, and then you offer your "friendly?" advice. Who are you? A demon or an angel? But you know what? I think you're still figuring it out, ain't you?'

'I'm just doing everything I can for the sake of justice.'

'Ah, right. And what's that? What is justice?'

'In terms of criminal law, it's simple. If you commit a crime, you pay for it.'

'What about other crimes? Kicking children out of their homes? Fucking women for a penny because they can't get any decent job? Condemning the poor and sick to workhouses to pick apart old rope for the rest of their days?'

'Damn it, Rose, you killed a man! What do you think happens next? Hmm? In your perfect world, where all children and women are safe, what happens to someone who commits a murder? What? Will it be right to just let murderers get away with it? Just because life turned out tough for them? Well, boo-hoo. Life is tough for everyone. If you have to resort to murder because you can't find a way to make a decent life for yourself, you go to prison. It's as simple as that. So now you will either tell me where your brother is, or they will hang you.'

'I don't know,' Rose mumbled.

'What is that?'

'I don't know where he is.'

'Was it he who killed Gummidge?'

'I won't answer that.'

'Suit yourself. I respect your wish to protect your brother. I envy you have a family you are ready to sacrifice yourself for. Not everyone is as lucky as you are.'

Rose raised a surprised look at Cassandra. Perhaps she had never thought of herself as one of the lucky ones.

'I have only one more question and then I'll leave you be,' the detective said, putting the cigarette case back into her purse. 'You've done a great job with all this ghost travesty. You even took the trouble of fetching my mother's ring to make me believe in the supernatural. But how did you know about it?'

The inmate's face, oddly naked without glasses, frowned.

'Your mother's ring? I don't know anything about it.'

'Come on, Rose. You can tell me now. It won't make things any worse for you. The ring, three rubies and a sprinkle of diamonds. The one you got out of my mother's grave.'

'We just wanted to scare you. What's the big deal? You still got the ring. We didn't keep it.'

'Well, thanks for that.'

It was a relief to know there was a mundane, earthly explanation as to how a piece of jewellery could have travelled all the way from the north to London and end up at Cassandra's feet as she walked in the cemetery.

'All right. I must go.' The detective got to her feet, trying to sound matter-of-factly and not give away how shaken she was from this whole ordeal.

'Will you be looking for Fredrick?' Rose seemed small again, like that frail secretary that was once introduced to the detective, wrapped in the old-fashioned shawl.

'I don't know. Probably.'

The inmate nodded, accepting the truth and inevitability of everything.

'Can I ask you for something?'

'What is it?'

'My glasses broke when they brought me here. Without them, I can barely see.'

Pity is a strange thing. Even those who commit terrible crimes can evoke such an emotion in the moment of their weakness.

'I'll see what can be done. Goodbye, Rose.'

When the gates of the prison were left behind her, Cassandra leaned on the ragged stone wall of the sombre building, suddenly overwhelmed with sorrow. This victory, this arrest, brought no triumph. And the notion of justice seemed ever so confusing.

* * *

Cassandra returned to Soho. At the entrance to the house, a swarm of children surrounded her, buzzing and jumping around like crickets, making faces as usual. Little Odie showed the greatest dedication to the shameless pantomime and got his shilling from the generous neighbour. He stared at the coin. The others craned their necks, trying to see over Odie's shoulders. It was more than she had ever given them before.

'I hope you'll be a kind boy and give this coin to your mother,' Cassandra told him.

The landlord, Mr Todd, slipped out from his room, drawing his housecoat tightly around himself, a little too late to hide from sight his yellowish drawers, loose at the knees and bottom.

'Here's a letter for you, Miss Ayers,' he said.

Cassandra tried not to gag at the reek of fried liver seeping out from the open door of Mr Todd's room.

'Thank you.' Her eyes darted to the envelope. Written in unfamiliar hand, it read *62 Pont Street, Knightsbridge*. 'Who brought it?'

'A young lady. She called herself Margie Ricket.'

The detective thanked Mr Todd, whose pasty face radiated some simple-minded glee from being useful, and set off for her room. Entering the chamber, she pulled out the gigantic pin securing her hat to her hair and tossed the hat on top of a pile of books and papers.

She scratched her scalp, itching after a day of wearing her hat, and opened the envelope. Inside, there was a short note, written by Margie herself, as well as another envelope. The note said:

I am very sorry, Miss Ayers. I found this letter only yesterday – it was in another box which belonged to my father. I hope it will help you in your investigation.

Clearly, Margie wasn't aware that the investigation was now closed. Cassandra opened the envelope anyway and read:

My dear Nathan,
Our friends Victor Deverill, Felix Aubert and Otto Calvert have arrived with their baggage. We thought three guest rooms would be enough, but then Clarence Corringham surprised us with his visit.
Nevertheless, we managed to accommodate all of them next to each other. Our house has very narrow beds, but the place is pleasantly quiet in the highest point of the park.
As I promised, I have kept our plan secret from our father. We have never had a good relationship with him, and now I doubt I can ever trust him.
With love,
O.I.

'Idiot!' Cassandra gasped, immediately realising her own mistake. She grabbed her hat and lunged for the door.

On her way downstairs, she stopped at Mr Todd's door and knocked feverishly. Seconds dragged by.

'Come on! Come on!' She thudded her fist against the rotting wood.

'Miss Ayers!' Mrs Cox poked her head out from under the stairs. She was approaching with her open palm extended. In it, she was carrying one shilling. 'I don't s'pose my little cheeky devils stole it from you?'

'Not now, Mrs Cox, please,' Cassandra abandoned the

attempts to reach out to her landlord and continued down the stairs. The red-faced woman followed.

'It's one shilling. Good money. So I decided I'd ask.'

'I gave it to them. It's yours now.'

'Goodness. What's all the fuss about, love?' Mrs Cox was huffing and puffing keeping up with her neighbour, who, despite her bad leg, turned out to be quite agile in her haste.

'Since Mr Todd is not here...'

'He went to the Three Crowns. Will return pie-eyed, don't you doubt.

'...I could use your help.'

'Ask anything, love.'

'Can Harry or any other of your children get to 24 Orchard Street as quick as they can?'

'Oh, that pack will do anything for you!'

'Here.' Cassandra gave her some more coins. 'They can get a cab.'

'Won't they love that!?'

'At 24 Orchard Street there's a photo studio. I want them to find Valentine Duvar and tell him that I need his immediate help at Highgate Cemetery. Can you repeat that?'

The woman's red face expressed intense thinking.

'Forty-two Orchard...'

'Twenty-four, Mrs Cox!'

'Right! Twenty-four Orchard Street. Ask for Valentine Duvar.'

'Thank you!' The detective proceeded to the exit, already waving at the cab that was passing by. 'It's a matter of life or death!'

In a moment, she disappeared inside the cab.

'Harry!' Mrs Cox called. 'Come here at once, you little rascal! I need you to go to 42 Orchard Street!'

The cab driver drove the horses at a spanking pace, but time dragged, and the scenes of London that went in and out of the window frame did not move quickly enough. The detective knocked on the side of the cab, again and again, asking the driver to go faster. He yelled back that he knew how to get the best from 'is 'orses! When they finally arrived, Cassandra jumped out of the cab before it had come to a stop.

'Wait for me here!' she said to the driver, pushing her way through a funeral train that was squeezing into the cemetery through the arch between two chapels. Men and women, dressed like a murder of black crows, followed a richly adorned hearse to bid their final farewell to someone of obvious high status.

The detective entered the burial grounds through the Colonnade and saw the grooves in the ground left by the wheel of a barrow. There were a number of them, coiling, overlapping and parting. Cassandra trotted along the grooves, leading her to the Terrace Catacombs.

...we managed to accommodate all of them next to each other. Our house has very narrow beds, but the place is pleasantly quiet in the highest point of the park.

Omer Ingleton had been deliberately writing in riddles, so that in the event the letter was read by the head of the Order, Baron Hexam, a man surely despised by the other members of the Order who had plotted against him, he would not be able to understand where the treasure had been hidden. In the text of the letter, Ingleton had called Magister Hexam *father*:

As I promised, I have kept our plan secret from our father. We have never had a good relationship with him, and now I doubt I can ever trust him.

That's why Baron Hexam didn't know about the treasure.

Narrow beds in the highest point of the park could only refer to the catacombs, in front of which the grooves from the barrow ended.

Cassandra entered, stepping carefully and silently. No one was around, except the dead lying in their coffins, their ornate burial boxes exposed to the curious eyes of visitors.

She moved stealthily along the wall until she found the niche bearing the name of *Clarence Corringham,* one of the friends mentioned in Ingleton's letter. His niche was empty, as were the two next to it. The stone covers, which once hid the insides of these loculi, lay at Cassandra's feet, shattered. One bore the name

Felix Aubert, another of Ingleton's friends from the letter. Marks in the layer of dust on the floor of each loculus indicated the coffins had been recently removed.

Ed Brockington, aka Fredrick Wharton, had fooled all of them. He had robbed the catacombs right under their noses, and transported the treasure away in his wheelbarrow while she and Mr Redlaw were having their last walk at the cemetery.

'What an idiot I am!' Cassandra paced the catacombs, her mind wringing itself out like a sponge as she tried to sort all of it. Reviewing the list of names again, she stopped in front of the crypt of *Otto Calvert.* Unlike the others, it remained untouched. She stepped forward to look at the crypt more closely.

Something cracked behind her back. Everything happened like in a nightmare, where she tried to run away from a monster hiding in her father's study, but her body refused to obey her. She tried to turn around quickly at the sound of the cracking, but then, suddenly, her head was struck a mighty blow from behind. She reeled from the force, and the catacombs swayed around her before she blacked out.

* * *

It was hard to breathe. It seemed there was an anvil on her chest.

Cassandra opened her eyes to see nothing but red circles growing in the darkness before her eyes. A circle grew and dissolved, giving birth to a new one. The cycle repeated endlessly.

After exploring the darkness, the detective determined she was lying in a horizontal position in a dark place with little air. Her lungs felt squeezed to the size of an apple. A terrible realisation flashed in her mind. Fumbling in the dark, she reluctantly confirmed her suspicions. The place she was locked in was nothing else but a coffin.

'No, no, no, no. It can't be true,' she whispered. A hysterical laugh escaped her throat. 'This can't be happening to me twice. What are the odds?'

She pushed on the lid, but it didn't yield an inch. She tried again with both hands and knees. No result.

Panic swelled in her stomach, heavy and rough like a stone. And it was getting bigger. Cassandra clenched her fists. She was not going to panic. With a tiny trembling exhalation, she let the panic out. She breathed in shallow breaths to conserve air as she thought over possible ways to escape, but her brain was failing her, revolving around only one thought: she was going to suffocate to death.

Feeling the surroundings for any possible way to escape, Cassandra came across her walking stick. It lay next to her, with its panther head at her feet. She pulled the stick closer and positioned its muzzle against the side of the coffin above her head. Her legs twitched as she contorted herself. The lack of air was getting unbearable. She was slowly suffocating.

At the moment she drifted out of her consciousness, an incredible thing happened to her. A piece of memory long forgotten suddenly flashed in her mind, so vivid and painful, it was as if it had happened only the day before.

Sunny day. Little Cassie tosses the hat away. It infuriates her nanny. 'We don't want freckles on this beautiful face!' But the sun is gentle. Cassie runs across the field. One thistle, one ground ivy, two cross-leaved heaths, one dandelion for her sweet mummy.

'We don't pick nettle,' little Cassie says to herself. 'It stings.'

And now she runs back home as fast as she can, clutching her tiny bunch of flowers. Her hand gets sweaty and absorbs the smell of the flowers. Cassie enters the coolness of the house, smelling her palm.

'Where's Mummy?'

'I haven't seen her since yesterday evening, little lady,' the maid says. 'I will check her room.'

'I'll do it myself!'

Two steps at a time! The stairs are so old and creaky. As Cassie jumps on them, they squeak. Mummy's bedchamber is right there, around the corner. The best bedchamber in the county! That's what the lady's maid thinks, so proud to serve in such a fine manor.

'Mummy!'

Cassie slaps her palm on the door rather than knock on it. It hurts her little hand when she knocks. The door handle is stiff, but Cassie manages to pull it down. A click, that melodic sound that invites the girl into her mother's room and her tight embrace.

'Mummy!'

And there she is, by the window. Waltzing. She is so graceful, she soars in the air.

'I brought you flowers, Mummy!'

Cassie steps into the room. Her mother doesn't turn to her. She is swaying. From left to right. Such a strange dance. Cassie raises her eyes. Her mother is hanging by a rope like a puppet on a string pulled by a puppeteer.

The girl's little feet approach. She takes her mother by the skirt and turns her. The chandelier from which Mummy is hanging chimes. Her mother's face is no longer beautiful; instead, it is blue. And her tongue is sticking out of her blackened mouth. Cassie screams.

'Merciful Lord!' the maid gasps as she catches up with the girl. She grabs Cassie and carries her out of the room.

One last desperate gasp for air returned Cassandra to life. She lay in the coffin, quietly sobbing, traumatized by the memory that had resurfaced stronger than ever before.

'Come on, softie. No time for tears.'

All she needed was one shot. Luckily, she had loaded the gun after she shot Rose Wharton. Yet, the coffin was too narrow; she would have needed to double up to press the trigger near the head of the walking stick. She moved her feet into one corner and bent her knees just a little more. Her bad, stiff leg screamed in protest. The tips of her fingers were almost there. Almost.

What if she wasn't in the catacombs? What if Wharton had buried her under the ground? If she shot a hole in the coffin, she would still not get any air. No, that's impossible. Wharton wouldn't have had time enough to bury her. Or would he? She had no inkling as to how long she'd been unconscious.

Finally, Cassandra managed to place the stick so that she could reach the trigger with her finger. She checked where the muzzle was aiming, then closed her eyes, a stupid reaction which would not save her from getting killed in case of a ricochet. She held her breath and pulled the trigger. A bang and a crack of wood. The weapon wasn't powerful, but still, the shot deafened her. Cassandra clenched her head. The ringing in her ears was so overwhelming it felt like it would split her head in half. Cassandra moaned with pain.

A saving stream of cold air brushed her face. She greedily gasped for it through the finger-wide hole. The ringing in her ears receded. Still, there was no light coming in through the opening. What if she really was in the ground or in a crypt? Cassandra strained her ears. Crickets were singing. It was night already.

The hole from the shot was too small to offer any help of escape. Her walking-stick gun had only one round, so now it was of no use.

'Hey!' she shouted. 'I'm here! Help!'

She waited. The cemetery gave no response. An owl stopped hooting and flew away. The dying sound of its wings beating the night air made her desperate.

'No! Don't leave!'

Cassandra pummelled the sides of the coffin. She poked through the shot-hole with a finger. There was no way she could widen it.

'I have a knife!' she suddenly recalled.

Yet, hidden in her boot, it was too far to reach. She contorted herself, reaching out for it. In vain.

Out of despair, Cassandra beat at the lid with her palms until they hurt, but then, a slight movement at her feet made her stop. There was something at the bottom of the coffin. A rat? An insect? Or some other pest? She reached out for the knife once again. No use.

The thing at her feet moved again and started crawling up her ankle. The woman shrieked at the top of her lungs when suddenly the coffin was yanked out of the loculus. It landed roughly onto the stone floor of the catacombs. The wooden sides collapsed from the impact and exposed her.

Shrieking and squealing, Cassandra rolled over and extracted herself out of the coffin. A rat, furry devil, skittered out of sight. She rested for a moment before realising she was lying at Valentine's and Mr Redlaw's feet. She immediately leveraged herself up onto her hands and knees, dismissing their help.

'I say! What's happened?' The superintendent picked up the cane with the panther head and gave it to her.

Fixing her dress, Cassandra tried not to look at Valentine, who was putting every effort into stifling a laugh.

'It was Fredrick Wharton. He hit me on the head and locked me in there.'

'What a dreadful thing! Are you hurt?'

Cassandra touched her head and felt a big goose-egg of a bump.

'Not really,' she lied, wincing slightly. 'Can't say the same about my dignity.'

Valentine burst into laughter.

'I'm sorry. It's... it's... one of my weird streaks. I just start laughing whenever someone... you know... trips or...' another bout of laughter seized him.

'How very Christian of you,' Cassandra replied. 'Why the bloody hell did it take you so long? I sent the boys after you ages ago.'

'Don't blame me. Your little messenger pigeons got the address wrong.'

'Ugh. I'll kill Mrs Cox,' Cassandra said, as she brushed some dirt from her dress. 'Anyway, thank you for coming to my rescue.'

'Mm-hmm,' Valentine said through pursed lips, still trying to stifle laughter.

'We need to bring you to the house and call for a doctor.' Mr Redlaw took her by her elbow.

'No. Not now. Wharton might still be here. We need to find him.'

They ran to the gates of the cemetery just in time to see a heavily loaded horse wagon leaving.

'There!' Valentine pointed at it as it disappeared around the corner.

'It's him.' Cassandra picked up a piece of red fake sideburns from the cobbled road.

Mr Redlaw whistled at the cab on the other side of the road. The cabman answered the signal and pulled up in front of them.

'Follow that wagon!' he commanded, as the three of them got inside.

The cab hurtled through the maze of streets, thrusting the passengers from one side to the other. It cut the corners easily and soon caught up with the wagon loaded with a bulky burden.

Valentine hung from the window watching the chase.

'Don't let him get away!' he shouted at the cabman who answered with a curse.

Suddenly, a gunshot rang between the two rows of buildings lining the street. Valentine ducked and hid inside. The cabman burst into swearing. Another bullet zipped over the cab and the cabman fell silent. His body rolled over the roof and tumbled onto the road, to the horrified screams of onlookers.

The three passengers exchanged a bewildered look. Mr Redlaw kicked open the door and climbed onto the cabman's seat as the cab dashed towards the market stalls. He picked up the reins and swerved into the lane, avoiding a collision. But the cab was thrashed mercilessly between the buildings, shattering the lanterns, extinguishing their lights. The door Mr Redlaw had climbed through and left open was taken off clean, and now house dwellers, disturbed by the racket, peeked out of their windows, right at the exposed passengers of the cab from hell.

More gunshots zipped over the cab, biting off pieces of bricks from the buildings and sending shrapnel in all directions.

'Damn! How many bullets has he got!?' Valentine shouted as he carefully poked his head out of the cab, where his face promptly met with a pub sign. He fell onto the floor, holding his face and moaning.

Cassandra retrieved a metal pillbox and shook it near her ear. The thing rattled. When she opened it, there was only one bullet inside. Another gunshot ripped through the front of the cab while she was trying to load the bullet into the American contraption in her cane.

The cab wrestled through the densely built-up lanes and the chase continued along the Regent's Canal.

'Hold me!' The detective leaned out and hung precariously from the doorway. Valentine took a firm grip on the handle near the door and hooked his other arm around her.

'I'm holding you!'

She took aim at Wharton. He was not too far and well-lighted by the moonlight. His weather-beaten face turned and he shot at his pursuers again. Crates full of treasures behind his back thundered as if guarding off anyone who would dare lay their hands on them.

'Shoot him! What are you waiting for?' Valentine shouted.

Head? No. A pile of gold is not worth a human life. Shoulder? She has only one round. Cassandra aimed at Wharton's hand and pulled the trigger. The perpetrator yelped and lost the reins as the bullet pierced the back of his hand. His left hand pulled at the other side of the reins, sending the wagon astray, until the horse, neighing madly, crashed into the flimsy railing and tumbled into the canal.

The dark waters hungrily swallowed the wagon with the treasure. A wild neighing of the drowning horse echoed in the stone bed of the canal. Two young men from an approaching boat jumped into the water to free the animal. An ancient captain stood on the nose of the boat, scowling at Fredrick Wharton, whose head was bobbing on the surface like a ripe apple.

'Damn drunkards.' The captain spat into the water.

Cassandra, Valentine and Mr Redlaw climbed down from the cab and approached the broken railing. A distant police whistle and a revving engine were getting closer. Wharton looked daggers at his pursuers. There was nowhere he could hide.

'Good grief!' the superintendent exclaimed, only now realising what havoc they had wrought.

'We got him.' Valentine sounded incredulous.

'Yes. We got him.' The detective looked at her partner. Two huge dark bruises had appeared around his eyes, an unfortunate consequence of his collision with the pub sign. Valentine resembled a panda bear. She doubled over, laughing.

'What?' he asked, when the superintendent chimed in.

'I get it now, why it's so funny when someone gets hurt,' Cassandra said.

CHAPTER 19

A Ghostly Hand

The case of a sister and brother plundering the Highgate Cemetery made the front page of all the newspapers of the Empire. On October 22, 1900, from Toronto to Calcutta, everyone was reading at breakfast about the two siblings hunting for the long-lost treasure of the secret Order.

Since the details of the investigation were not fully revealed, the public made the wildest assumptions about the Whartons' intentions that, according to some more romantic readers, were "quite noble," for the two thugs were, arguably, going to donate all the stolen riches to an orphanage. That made them almost Robin Hoods in the eyes of the poor and miserable.

The interest in the case was fueled even more by a sensational article in the Daily Telegraph about a lady detective who put an end to the Whartons' little adventure. They called her Lady C. Judging from how much familiar detail there was in an accompanying sketch, in which Cassandra was holding Rose at gunpoint in the middle of an elegantly furnished drawing room, she had no doubt the "reliable source" mentioned in the article was none other than Mrs Redlaw.

Philip Ingleton was released from custody soon after they arrested Fredrick Wharton. Neither of the Ingletons thanked Cassandra for her help in the investigation. Soon after, they sent their butler, Ogbourne, with a cheque for her. The old man squeamishly entered her house and handed her the cheque, with a slight smile that was supposed to make up for the lack of gratitude from his masters.

In the weeks to come, the Whartons would stand trial. Fredrick would be found guilty of murder and sentenced to death by hanging. As for Rose, while being the brains of their criminal operation, she would be found guilty of theft and obstructing the investigation. She would be sentenced to twenty years in prison. She once said it always made her sad to look at the dates on the gravestones and count how many years a person lived. Well, when released in twenty years, Rose would be fifty-eight. That was the kind of arithmetic Cassandra found even more disheartening. Before her transfer to the place of detention, the detective would bring Rose a new pair of glasses. They would never meet again.

However, none of these events had occurred by the time Cassandra attended at the photo studio.

'Here you are.' Valentine handed her an envelope. The bruises around his eyes were dark purple now, making the resemblance to a panda particularly striking.

'I'm sorry. I can't look at your face without a good laugh,' she admitted, opening the packet of brown paper.

'I'm happy humour is not lost on you.'

The photograph inside the envelope was of herself, the one she intended to send to her family at Caxton Hall. It was good work. The photographer managed to capture the best features of her: a play of shadows on one side of her face, a slight turn of her head that complemented the shape of her nose and a gaze both soulful and wistful.

'You know, some believe a photograph has a piece of their soul,' Valentine said as he organized his equipment.

'What a shame it will be sent to Caxton. Not a single bit of me deserves to be locked in that place.'

Her words made him stop for a moment as he was putting the tripod into a wooden case.

'Home sweet home, right?' he snorted.

'Right. Wait a minute.' She raised the photograph to her eyes.

'What is this?'

'What?'

Valentine drew aside a heavy draping that was covering the only window, and bright but rather desaturated daylight flooded the room. They both craned over the photograph.

'I can't believe you tried to pull this trick on me,' Cassandra said. She pointed at her shoulder in the miniature depiction of herself. There, resting on her shoulder, was a very distinct but semi-transparent woman's hand, yet there was nobody in the photograph besides herself. A ghostly hand just floated there, absent a body. 'I thought I told you it was for my family.'

'Wait, wait, wait, wait.' Valentine peered at the picture. 'I didn't do anything to it. I swear to God! I didn't tamper with it.'

'You master of optical illusions.' She grabbed her purse and headed for the exit.

'No, no, no!' The photographer blocked her way, clinging to the doorway with all limbs like a spider, while trying to still study the picture in his hand. 'This is incredible. I think I finally caught it on camera.'

'Caught what?'

'A ghost.'

'Let me pass.'

'How can I prove it to you?'

'Well, you can't. Because ghosts do not exist.'

'Why can't you open your mind just a little? We are witnessing here something truly amazing.'

'You know what's amazing? Your audacity. Now, let me pass.'

'I know what we need! An experiment.'

'What?'

'I'll take one more photo of you. You'll watch every step of the process. If the hand doesn't appear this time, you win, and I accept there must have been some... technical malfunction.'

'That's what you call it?' Cassandra folded her arms. 'What happens if the hand appears again?'

'Well, that'll be much harder to explain. Also, it will take a few hours to develop the negatives.'

'All right. Let's do it,' she sighed.

'Good. Thank you.'

He rushed out of the room and started setting up the tripod. It gave her time to study the photograph more closely. And when she did, her heart sank.

'Mr Duvar,' she called out. 'I don't think we'll need your experiment.'

'What? Why?' he returned.

'I found the proof you didn't do it,' she whispered, feeling her world start to reel. 'At least, it'd be a very difficult thing for you to pull off.'

The ghostly hand that was resting on her shoulder in the photograph was wearing a ring with three rubies and a sprinkle of diamonds. It was her mother's ring. It was her mother's hand.

Whatever optical illusions Valentine was capable of, he certainly was not capable of raising the dead. Could it be, for whatever reason, they had raised themselves?

CASSANDRA'S SHADOWS

Cassandra's Shadows is a series of dark tales for lovers of Victorian mystery. Cassandra Ayers scandalises Victorian society as an out-of-place private detective who debunks paranormal phenomena. But the hardest to debunk is her own mysterious past.

The Highgate Ghost ✗

In Book 1 of the series, Cassandra Ayers embarks on a case of grave desecration at Highgate Cemetery allegedly haunted by a terrifying ghost; however, the most mysterious and frightening case she is challenged to solve lies in her own past. Maybe now, after Cassandra sees her mother's ghostly hand in her photo, she will be able to find the answers.

A Werewolf Of The Moor

In Book 2, a terrible murder happens on the Saddleworth Moor. A carriage driver and five of his passengers are killed by what seems like a beast with fangs and claws. Cassandra is asked to consult the police on this case. As she starts digging into the horrifying mass murder, she finds out about a political plot, blackmail and a gang called The Chameleons that are involved in this gruesome business. The case casts a shadow at her father, Lord Dunstan, the MP and one of the suspects.

✗ *quiet sufficient no need for more awful, see what you think.*

Printed in Great Britain
by Amazon

18199723R00099